MW01094279

"Jack's storyte   ...., and the
short-chapter s   ......y answer to Lay's potato chips:
you just want one more and before you know it, you've gone
through the whole thing.

- **David Bashore**
The Times-News, Twin Falls, ID

"Jack Patterson does a fantastic job at keeping you engaged and
interested. I look forward to more from this talented author."

- ***Aaron Patterson***
bestselling author of SWEET DREAMS

DEAD SHOT

"Small town life in southern Idaho might seem quaint and idyllic
to some. But when local newspaper reporter Cal Murphy begins
to uncover a series of strange deaths that are linked to a sticky
spider web of deception, the lid on the peaceful town is blown
wide open. Told with all the energy and bravado of an old pro,
first-timer Jack Patterson hits one out of the park his first time at
bat with *Dead Shot*. It's that good."

- ***Vincent Zandri***
bestselling author of THE REMAINS

"You can tell Jack knows what it's like to live in the newspaper
world, but with *Dead Shot*, he's proven that he also can write one
heck of a murder mystery. With a clever plot and characters you
badly want to succeed, he is on his way to becoming a new era
James Patterson."

- ***Josh Katzowitz***
NFL writer for CBSSports.com
& author of Sid Gillman: Father of the Passing Game

"Patterson has a mean streak about a mile wide and puts his two
main characters through quite a horrible ride, which makes for
good reading."

- ***Richard D.****, reader*

DEAD LINE

"This book kept me on the edge of my seat the whole time. I didn't really want to put it down. Jack Patterson has hooked me. I'll be back for more."

- Bob Behler
3-time Idaho broadcaster of the year
and play-by-play voice for Boise State football

"Like a John Grisham novel, from the very start I was pulled right into the story and couldn't put the book down. It was as if I personally knew and cared about what happened to each of the main characters. Every chapter ended with so much excitement and suspense I had to continue to read until I learned how it ended, even though it kept me up until 3:00 A.M.

- Ray F., reader

DEAD IN THE WATER

"In Dead in the Water, Jack Patterson accurately captures the action-packed saga of a what could be a real-life college football scandal. The sordid details will leave readers flipping through the pages as fast as a hurry-up offense."

- Mark Schlabach,
ESPN college sports columnist and
co-author of *Called to Coach*
and *Heisman: The Man Behind the Trophy*

THE WARREN OMISSIONS

"What can be more fascinating than a super high concept novel that reopens the conspiracy behind the JFK assassination while the threat of a global world war rests in the balance? With his new novel, *The Warren Omissions*, former journalist turned bestselling author Jack Patterson proves he just might be the next worthy successor to Vince Flynn."

- Vincent Zandri
bestselling author of THE REMAINS

DEAD AND GONE

A Cal Murphy Thriller

JACK PATTERSON

DEAD AND GONE
© Copyright 2015 Jack Patterson

First Print Edition 2014

Cover Design by Dan Pitts

Published in the United States of America
Hangman Books
Boise, Idaho 83714

*To Chris Beckham, a great friend and a man
who helped me understand the importance of NASCAR
while living in South Georgia*

3/2015

DEAD AND
GONE

To Paige,
Thanks for all your
help at the track!
Happy reading!

Jack Potter

CHAPTER 1

THE MAN YANKED THE BILL of his cap just above his eyes and hustled across the garage area teeming with cars prepped for today's race. He'd never killed anyone before nor did he have the stomach for it. However, he had no problem doing what it took to ensure his target ended up dead.

He fired up the blowtorch and looked over his shoulder. The locked garage ensured he could do his deed in peace. He slid the helmet visor down and began heating the part.

Endorphins coursed through his body while he watched the metal begin to glow. He'd waited long enough for this moment, one that required precision and a steady hand. Heat the part too much and he'd either have plenty of explaining to do or worse—utter failure. Heat it too little and he'd fail in a way that he couldn't accept.

Once he finished, he stopped and admired his handiwork.

Perfect.

He twirled the part with his gloved hand and then looked around the garage area just to make sure no one was around.

With the type of efficiency that would make the pit crew

team swell with pride, he put the part in place and tidied up the equipment.

He put his cap back on, jammed his hands in his jacket pockets, and stole across the grounds toward the garage exit. For good measure, he looked behind him for peace of mind. If he saw no one, he'd know if his work was true; he'd get away with it.

He didn't see anyone—but someone saw him.

***

CARSON TANNER PEERED at the inner workings of his Chevy SS racecar. In forty-five minutes, he'd zoom around the track at just under 200 miles per hour behind the thunder of a 750-horsepower engine. And while he had one of the best crews on the racing circuit, Tanner always preferred to poke his head under the hood one last time before driver introductions.

Pat "Dirt" Walter slid out from underneath the car. "What's the matter, Tanner? You don't trust us?"

Tanner shook his head. "I trust you with my life, Dirt, every weekend. Nothing wrong with takin' a peek, is there?"

Dirt grunted and slid back underneath the car.

Tanner stroked the car as he walked toward the backend. Lost in thought, he nearly tripped over another crew member, Russ Ross, who was running through his last-minute checklist.

"I hope your head's in the game today," Ross said. "We need this one."

Tanner nodded. "I'm ready. Don't you worry."

He circled the car once again before Sylvia Yates placed

her hand on his back.

"Ready to meet little Ella?" she asked.

Tanner nodded and followed the spunky brunette who served as the media relations director for the Davis Motorsports team.

"She's not feeling well today, but I think you're gonna love her," Sylvia said over her shoulder as they walked toward the team's hauler.

Tanner wiped his brow with his sleeve. "Gotta love Texas in October," he said.

"Yeah, and that's why we're meeting inside," Sylvia said as she led him inside the hauler's cramped air-conditioned quarters.

Ella's parents stood up and introduced themselves the moment they saw Tanner enter the room.

"Mr. Tanner!" a young girl squealed as she jumped up into his arms.

He leaned back and grinned at the freckle-faced eight-year-old now comfortable in his arms. She grabbed his golden-colored hat with the number thirty-nine stitched onto the front and put it on.

"You must be Ella," he said. "Just call me Carson. Are you ready?"

She nodded and smiled as they climbed into the back of a pickup truck for the parade lap. She twisted the hat on her head. "Are you gonna put Cashman into the wall today?"

"I like you already."

"Well, are you?"

Tanner looked her square in the eyes as he broke into another grin. "If I have to, I will. Don't you worry. I'm gonna win this race today, just for you."

Ella clapped and squealed again before giving him a hug. "You're the best!"

Tanner laughed as she nearly fell down in the back of the truck. "Hold on, honey!"

She regained her balance and started to discuss race strategies with him.

"Hartman's been runnin' real good lately, but he's never done well in Texas," she said. "I think you can take him."

Tanner arched his eyebrows. "Even though Hartman won the pole?"

"Poles don't mean anything. My daddy says poles are nothing but a Sunday afternoon drive through the hills. If you ain't tradin' paint, you might as well be drivin' a bus."

"Any other advice?"

"Yeah, watch out for Cashman on turn three. He's wrecked there the past five times he's run here. And he's got nothin' to lose, especially since he's behind you in the standings. If he doesn't catch you, his season is done, so be careful around him."

Tanner nodded and tousled her short brown hair. "How'd you learn so much about racing?"

"My dad. It was about the only thing we could watch on the weekends in the summer when I was getting chemo. We'd sit in the chemo lounge and watch all the races together. I got hooked."

"Well, you're a brave little girl. It takes more courage to do what you're doing than it does to drive a race car around a track, that's for sure."

Ella shook her head. "I'd be scared to drive a car that fast, Mr. Tanner. You have to get in the car yourself. But cancer comes and gets you. You don't have a choice. I'm certainly not gonna just sit around and feel sorry for myself. I've still got a lotta life to live."

Tanner fought to hold back the tears welling up in his eyes. "You have an incredible attitude—and you're right, you have a lotta livin' to do. Keep fightin'."

The lap ended and they climbed out of the truck and rejoined Ella's family.

Tanner looked up at her parents. Ella's mother dabbed at the mascara streaking down her cheeks. Her father, sporting a No. 39 shirt, scratched at the corner of his eye and looked away.

He looked back at Ella. "You ready to go help me get into my car?"

"Am I ready? It's all I've ever wanted to do since I started following you."

"Well, all right then. Let's go."

Sylvia led the entourage toward the platform where NASCAR conducted driver introductions. She stood with Ella's parents on the track while Ella walked with Tanner up the steps on the backside of the stage at the starting line. As Tanner waited for his name to be called, Todd Cashman walked up behind him.

"Tanner, did ya finally find someone who can teach you how to drive?" Cashman said.

"Come on, Cashman. She's a kid," Tanner said.

Ella stamped her foot and put her hands on her hips. "Maybe you need to find someone to teach you some manners, Mr. Cashman."

"Nobody told me it was take-a-brat-to-work day," he snipped.

"I hope you run out of gas five feet from the finish line,"

Ella said.

Tanner gently rubbed Ella's back. "Now, Ella, let's not be ugly."

"And in the Number 39 car, Carson Tanner!" boomed the announcer over the loudspeaker, interrupting their spat.

"Now, if you'll excuse us," Tanner said.

Tanner held Ella's hand as they walked onto the front of the stage to a roar. He waved and encouraged Ella to do the same.

"And in the Number 7 car, Todd Cashman!" the announcer said.

Tanner leaned down. "That's our cue to leave, Ella." He led her down the steps and to his car parked on pit road.

Once he was out of earshot, he leaned over again and whispered in her ear. "I'm definitely gonna put Cashman into the wall now."

She giggled and twirled as they continued toward the car.

Tanner's crew chief Owen Burns met them at their pit. Burns worked over a toothpick in his mouth as he tilted his head and looked into his driver's eyes.

"You've got the best car out there today, kid," Burns said. "If you don't win, it's all on you."

"No pressure," Tanner said.

"We need this win—and I know you can do it. Just get out there and race your heart out."

Tanner patted Burns on the shoulder and kept walking toward his car.

Ella tugged on Tanner's arm. "I know you can do it, too," she said.

He'd almost forgotten she was there, already lost in his thoughts about the race. Burns didn't need to say a word.

He knew he had the best car and he knew anything but a win would suffice if he expected to advance in the championship chase.

Tanner zeroed in on his car, but stopped just short at the sight of his wife, Jessica. They'd been married less than a year and it was nothing short of bliss. He told his dad he could handle everything about the lifestyle of the circuit— except for the loneliness. "I'm surrounded by hundreds of people, but I often feel like no one knows I exist," he told a pretty young woman one night at a meet-and-greet with fans. It wasn't a pick-up line either. He was just pouring out his heart to a person who seemed to enjoy listening. That was Jessica. And now she stood next to his car waiting to give him a good luck kiss.

Tanner embraced her and gave her a long kiss. Then he held her as she lingered in his arms.

"Knock 'em dead out there today," she said as she picked at his uniform.

"I'll do my best."

"Burns said you've got the best car out there and that you ought to win."

"I certainly don't wanna disappoint anyone." He slid his hand over her pooching belly. "Especially you two."

She smiled. "We need to get you a new suit." She picked at few loose threads. "This one's coming apart."

He sighed. "Just tape it up. This one is fine. Besides, it's my good luck suit. I was wearing this the day I met you."

She kissed him again. "Go get 'em."

He climbed into the car as his crew began helping him with the safety belts and HANS device.

Jackson Holmes, another one of Tanner's crew

members, yanked on a few of Tanner's straps. "Don't screw it up. We need this one today."

Tanner flashed him a thumbs up.

"Check, one, two," Burns said over the 39 car's radio frequency. "Can you hear me, Tanner?"

"Loud and clear."

"Good. Now just be smart out there today and you'll be fine."

Tanner glanced back at his team, all giving him the thumbs up sign. He waved at Ella, who jumped up and down and clapped.

"Let's do this."

Country music star Luke Bryan crooned the National Anthem before Major League hall of fame pitcher Nolan Ryan took the mic. "Drivers, start your engines."

Tanner fired up his car, drowning out the roar from the crowd.

He followed the pace car onto the track and began to visualize himself on each and every turn. Visualization was a trick his father taught him years ago to help ease his mind while playing baseball. "If you see yourself going through the motions, they'll become second nature to you, son," he'd said. "Then you can concentrate on the details that will take you from good to great."

Tanner wasn't a great driver yet, but there was little doubt that he was already a good one on his second year in NASCAR's highest circuit. He claimed rookie of the year honors last season and could qualify for one of the final four spots in the championship chase with a win today. While winning for his team was important, in thirty minutes Ella had stolen his heart—and he wanted to win for her more than anyone else.

"One to go. Green flag next time around. Be ready," Burns said over the radio.

Tanner zoned in and gripped the wheel tighter. The hum of the 43 cars on the track turned to a roar.

"Green, green, green," said the team's spotter perched atop the luxury suites.

Tanner jammed his foot on the gas and focused on finding his line heading into turn one. He remained oblivious to the crowd rising to their feet and cheering as the race officially got underway.

The race remained uneventful for the most part. Only a handful of cautions and two wrecks had slowed down what was otherwise turning out to be a fast race. Tanner, who'd started second, had drifted back to no lower than eighth over the past 300 laps but had surged to third behind Cashman and Garrett Hillman.

When Buzz Goff spun out on lap 310, all the teams on the lead lap pulled in for a pit stop.

"What are we doin'?" Tanner asked.

"You're takin' four tires," Burns said.

"You sure that's a good idea? We might lose what we've worked so hard to get here."

"Just trust me, kid. It'll work out."

When the pit stop concluded, Tanner zipped back onto the track in ninth place.

"I hope you made a good call, Burns. I'm not likin' this."

"Just be smart. You'll see."

On lap 315, Tanner passed two drivers to move up to seventh. Three laps later, he passed two more. By lap 320, he was sitting on Cashman's tail.

"Fourteen more laps," Burns said. "Just be patient and wait for the right moment to make your move."

For the next ten laps, Tanner remained poised to take advantage of any opening he could get to slip past Cashman. The lapped traffic made it more difficult than he thought. And then there was another caution.

"What is it this time?" Tanner asked.

"Debris on the roadway," Burns said.

"Imagine that. NASCAR wants a green-white-checkered finish."

"You've got the fresher tires. Cashman only took two."

Tanner chuckled. "Let's hope that's his undoin'." He still wanted to put Cashman into the wall.

Tanner watched the pace car peel off into the pits.

"Green, green, green," the spotter said.

It's now or never.

Tanner jammed his foot on the gas and edged his way past Cashman on the outside of the back straightaway.

"Clear, clear, clear," the spotter said.

"Good job," Burns said. "Keep it up, kid."

Tanner drifted down in front of Cashman and started to pull away. He sped through turn four and down the front straightaway. Out of the corner of his eye, he saw the crowd rising to its collective feet as the white flag waved, signaling the final lap.

"Just keep it steady, and you've got this race," Burns said.

Tanner felt adrenaline surge through his body. Though he'd never touched drugs, he couldn't imagine any high surpassing what he felt in this moment. He'd all but vanquished his archrival and secured a spot in the championship chase in Miami for the season's final race.

He whipped through turn two. The 39 car was running the best it had ever run.

Burns words crackled over the radio. "You got this. Bring it home."

As Tanner approached turn three, he took his foot off the gas, but nothing happened. He stomped on the gas, hoping to free up the stuck throttle.

"The throttle's stuck!" Tanner said.

Burns watched in horror.

Tanner jammed his foot on the brake. Everything but the car slowed down. Impact with the wall remained imminent in less than a second, but it felt like a minute to Tanner with frightful anticipation.

Wham!

Traveling at just over 195 miles per hour, the 39 car slammed into the wall. Debris flew everywhere as the crunch of metal and squeal of tires echoed throughout Texas Motor Speedway. That was followed by a collective gasp from the crowd—and then an explosion.

Safety and rescue crews sped toward the accident as the trailing drivers navigated the pieces strewn across the track.

Everyone watched and waited for Tanner to emerge from the car.

They waited and waited and waited.

Then another explosion.

The rescue team hosed down the flaming car, extinguishing the flames, and began to cut open the crumpled driver's side. An ambulance pulled in front, blocking the view of most spectators and crew members. Only grainy shots from a helicopter overhead kept fans and race teams apprised of what was happening.

NASCAR officials declared the race over and Cashman the winner.

With Tanner's status unknown, Cashman refused to miss his chance to celebrate, burning out his tires near the finish line under a deafening chorus of boos.

"Give me somethin'," Burns said to NASCAR officials. "We gotta know what's going on."

Several moments of silence followed. Then a NASCAR official answered him.

"He's gone."

CHAPTER 2

CAL MURPHY RUSHED out of the pit area to view the action on Big Hoss, the enormous HD screen that sprawled along the infield of the track opposite the grandstands by the finish line. He tuned in on his headset to find out what was happening. With the flashing lights of emergency vehicles on one end of the track, Cashman burning out at the other, and a disapproving crowd in between, Cal tried to piece things together.

He took his headphones off and asked one of the men standing next to him, "What happened?"

"Tanner had it won but crashed on turn three," the man replied. "And Cashman is just being a jerk—like always."

Cal slipped his headphones back on and tried to find out the status of Tanner. Nothing but concern and questions. No answers from any of the official channels.

Once Cashman's car wobbled off the track, silence fell on the crowd as they all stood up and stared at the activity near turn number three.

Cal hustled inside the media center, the only semi-quiet place near the track where reporters could escape. He watched on the monitors as they ripped off the door to Tanner's car and prepared to move his body.

"That doesn't look good," one of the reporters quipped.

Everyone froze and looked at the screens. Cal noticed several reporters wince at the sight of Tanner's limp body as medical workers hoisted him onto a stretcher.

Cal's phone buzzed. He glanced at the screen and saw it was Max Folsom, his editor from the Charlotte Observer.

"Are you watching this?" Cal said as he answered.

"I think he's dead, Cal," Folsom said.

"Are you serious?"

"I haven't seen anybody hit the wall that hard since Jimmy Gillespie smashed into Turn 3 at Talladega. And you know what happened to him."

"I've only seen the replays so far in slow motion, but it looked bad."

"Where were you?"

"In the pits, trying to interview Buzz Goff."

"Cal, that close to the end of the race? I know he's Charlotte's favorite son, but nothing trumps the finale. He wasn't going anywhere."

"Just trying to get you the story early."

"I appreciate the effort, but you shouldn't have been stuck in the pits when the most important part of the race was occurring—I don't care how many television angles you'll be able to see the replays from. Got it?"

Cal nodded. "Roger that. Still just getting used to this beat."

"It ain't football, that's for sure."

"I'm starting to get it. I know that rubbin', son, is racin'."

"I hope you haven't quoted Days of Thunder to anyone at the track. Real NASCAR people hate that movie."

"Are you droppin' the hammer on me?"

"Please stop with those quotes. Now, go get me a prize-winning story and don't make me regret subbing you in for Thompson."

Cal hung up and stared at the images filling the screens around the room. He'd covered plenty of marquee sporting events, but NASCAR still felt foreign to him. The sport opened its doors wide for fans and media alike, and it took Cal some time to get used to it. Open pits during the race was a new concept to him as well. There wasn't another sport where he could wander into a team's locker room and interview a player before the game was over. But he could in NASCAR. The minute a driver spun out and ended his day, it wasn't just the television reporters who could grab him for a few quotes—it was anyone with a proper pit pass.

If Cal had his druthers, he would've been in Atlanta this weekend, helping the Observer's coverage of the Carolina Panthers against the Falcons. But the paper's NASCAR beat writer, Hal Thompson, suffered a massive heart attack the month before and Cal drew the assignment of freshly minted auto racing scribe. Making things even more challenging for him was the fact that he'd never once attended a race before he started, much less covered one.

NFL scores crawled on the bottom of the screen. Falcons 45, Panthers 6.

I definitely got the better assignment today.

But it wasn't an easy one, not with Goff wrecking and eliminating himself from the championship chase—and now Charlotte-native Carson Tanner smashing into the wall on Turn 3 on the final lap.

At least I'll have plenty to write about.

Then the announcement came; Tanner was gone.

Several people in the media room groaned while others shouted "No!" Cal walked outside and listened as the moans of the crowd spread like a wave through the stands.

Tanner was easily one of the most popular drivers on the tour. Fans loved him, the media adored him, sponsors fought over him. And in an instant, Carson Tanner was dead.

Cal walked along pit road toward Tanner's crew and saw Tanner's wife, Jessica, retch. She pulled at her hair and doubled over, screaming and yelling.

Maybe I got the worst assignment today.

Any attempts to capture the raw emotion of the scene would leave him open to criticism, the kind Cal didn't like. Local sports talk radio in Charlotte would likely skewer him, creating an entire segment to analyze his sensitivity, or lack thereof. Yet he had no choice. This was the assignment. A cushy trip to Texas morphed into a nightmare for Cal. Carson Tanner was dead—and there was no way around it.

Then Jessica stood up. Cal stared at her silhouetted frame, outlined by the pronounced pooch from her stomach area. He'd forgotten she was pregnant.

Cal watched as one of the pit crew members helped Jessica down the ladder that accessed the perch overlooking pit road. She crumpled to the ground once she stepped off the ladder, pounding with her fist onto the asphalt. "Why? Why? Why?" she wailed.

It was an answer everyone wanted, but likely it was a simple one: mechanical failure.

It's not like Tanner would suddenly forget how to drive, not after rounding Turn 3 without incident 333 previous times that afternoon. Something went wrong at the absolute worst time — and it would remain a mystery for the time being. All that was known was the horrible news: Carson Tanner, at age 25, was dead.

Cal scrambled around pit road, gathering as much information as he could about the incident as well as comments from other drivers about the race itself. Despite the tragedy, there was still a story to write, albeit an overshadowed one.

Cashman, who was seconds away from virtual elimination with a Tanner victory, reasserted himself into the championship chase—a fact that nearly every fan bemoaned. He had now qualified for the finale in Miami, benefitting the most from the spectacular crash behind him. Cal acknowledged that no one could fault him since it wasn't something he did that caused Tanner to crash. But everyone could certainly resent Cashman for it, especially after Cal would report that Cashman burned off his tires near the finish line while the last breath escaped from Tanner. It provided the stark contrast about two of the most successful drivers during the tour. One beloved, the other reviled.

With all his interviews completed, Cal settled into his seat and typed his stories. First the story about the race itself, then the heavy one: Carson Tanner's crash and death.

In a short conversation with a teary-eyed Sylvia Yates, Cal learned that the girl who was with Tanner during driver introductions was a cancer patient named Ella, a girl fighting for her life who'd been connected with Tanner through the Make-a-Wish foundation. It wasn't anything Yates publicized, per Tanner's request. He told her he wanted to do good for good's sake, not to impress fans and the general public.

"That's just the kind of man that Tanner is," Sylvia had told Cal as she paused. "I mean, was."

Cal brushed a tear back from his own eyes while he typed. It was one thing to speak with an athlete who'd just experienced a season-ending injury, but it was another to ask questions about a man who had died just moments ago.

He finished the story and emailed it to his editor. He waited for confirmation that he'd received it. A text arrived fifteen minutes later:

"Good work, Cal."

He packed up his laptop and notes before heading out the door. The usual jovial mood writers shared as they finished up a weekend of race coverage was gone, replaced by a somber tone. Cal slipped out the door, content to let everyone process the tragic events without interruption.

He strolled through the pits, still bustling with activity. NASCAR checked racecars to make sure they were compliant. Those teams that had already finished were loading their cars onto their haulers and exiting as quickly as possible.

Cal stared at the scene, one that still seemed surreal in light of the race's tragic events. He remained oblivious to others around him as he took in the sights. Then someone bumped into him.

"What the—"

"Sorry," the man said. He kept walking without as much as a glance over his shoulder.

Cal jammed his hands in his pockets and felt a piece of paper he would've sworn wasn't there moments ago. He fished it out and unfolded it. He read it and put his hand over his gaping mouth:

"That crash was no accident."

CHAPTER 3

NED DAVIS SCOOTED across the pit area and disappeared inside the No. 39 Davis Motorsports Team hauler, which stretched about 80 feet. The throng of reporters clambering after him to get a quote about Carson Tanner's crash horrified him, almost as much as the accident itself. He knew eventually he'd have to say something and wanted to—but not now.

He skipped up the steps to the meeting area at the front of the truck. Shutting the door behind him, he leaned against it with a heavy sigh. He closed his eyes for a moment and then opened them to see his girlfriend, Alexa Jennings.

"Come to momma," she said, shifting into an upright position on the couch. "I think you need some lovin'."

Davis plopped down next to her and slouched on the sofa. Without warning, she grabbed him and buried his head into her chest.

Alexa stroked his head. "It's okay, papa bear. Everything is gonna be all right."

He pulled back and eyed her carefully. "Do you know what happened out there today?"

She nodded. "Just because I care more about you doesn't mean I'm insensitive. I thought of Tanner as my own son, but you're the one who needs comforting right now."

When Davis started dating Alexa a year and a half ago, comfort wasn't one of the traits that drew him to her. Her freakishly large bosom and piercing green eyes caught his attention first—and in that order.

Sufficiently drunk one evening at a strip club in Vegas, he tipped her more than she'd made in the previous two months. Before the end of the night, he propositioned her with something more intriguing than an invite to his hotel room.

"Join me on the road," Davis said.

She looked him up and down. "Honey, haven't you heard? What happens in Vegas stays in Vegas?"

"I want to take Vegas with me."

She climbed down off the stage and patted him on the head. "This is my home—and you're just a wee bit drunk."

He sat down and pulled out his checkbook and wrote a check for a hundred thousand dollars. He ripped it out and handed it to her. "Here. Is this enough to convince you to find a new home?"

Alexa told her boss that she was quitting and left with Davis. And while he knew she came because of the money, he believed she stayed because she loved him.

Here she was, consoling him and stroking his hair. This furthered Davis' suspicions that love was greater than money in their case. He appreciated that about her along with the facts that she was hot and didn't mind being seen with a man who was eight inches shorter than she was.

"Are you gonna be all right?" she asked as she caressed his arm.

He shook his head. "I don't know. It was just so awful.

I was near our pit when it happened and stayed there until we got that word that he was gone. When I saw Jessica thrashing around, I just couldn't handle it. I didn't know what to say to her. I'm just so numb."

"She'll be fine. She's a strong woman."

"But that kid? He'll come into this world without a father."

"You didn't have a father and you turned out just fine."

He sighed. "That's a matter of opinion. I'm not sure that my mother is looking down from heaven on me and thinking that she raised an outstanding man. I'm quite certain I'm not fine."

Alexa stamped her foot. "Now, listen, papa bear. Don't you believe that nonsense floating around in your head. You're more than outstanding. You're amazing and you need to know it."

He pulled back. "But you don't know what I've done."

"What? Frequenting strip clubs? Playing hardball in business ventures? Spreading rumors about competitors? None of that makes you a bad person."

"Then what does it make me?"

She stared at the ceiling for a moment and tapped her cheek with her finger. "It makes you an ambitious man who works hard and plays hard. Nothing wrong with that."

"I'm afraid it's my zealous ambition that has me feeling down at the moment."

"Why? Are you blaming yourself for Tanner's death? It's not your fault, you know."

"If I didn't own this race team—"

"Tanner would've died driving for someone else. It's a tough break, but it doesn't mean that you're responsible."

"Not directly, anyway."

"What are you trying to say?"

"Never mind. I just need to think about what I'm going to tell the press." He stood up and cracked the window. Craning his neck through the small opening, Davis noticed the gaggle of reporters outside his hauler had nearly doubled from the group that was following him earlier.

Sylvia Yates burst into the room. "Don't worry, Mr. Davis. You won't have to say anything to the press. I just wrote up this press release and want you to sign off on it so I can disseminate these reporters. Once we give them what they want, they'll leave you alone."

He stood up and hugged Sylvia. "Thank you. You have no idea the anxiety I was starting to feel."

Sylvia nodded and handed the media release to him. "It's a sad day for all of us, but I knew you especially wouldn't want to speak to the press in a time like this."

Davis scanned the paper and handed it back. "Go for it. This has my approval."

"Good. I'm hoping that once I give this to them, they'll leave us alone so we can all deal with this tragedy."

She opened the door and skipped down the steps and out of sight.

"See, it's getting better already," Alexa said.

Davis slumped back onto the couch. "I don't know if avoiding the press is making things better—it's just not making them any worse at the moment."

"Take the time you need to grieve. It'll be good for your soul." She shot him a wink and started to climb into his lap. "And I know just the thing that'll help—"

Davis' phone buzzed and he struggled to get away from

Alexa so he could answer it.

"Papa bear? Come on."

He held up his index finger as he looked at the name that flashed onto the screen. "I need to take this. Just excuse me for a minute."

Alexa understood what he meant and scurried out of the room.

"Elliot, thanks for calling," Davis began. "I was wondering when I might be hearing from you."

"How are you doing, man?"

"Not great at the moment. It's kind of surreal right now. You know how much I liked Tanner."

"I do, which makes me wonder why you're having such a difficult time right now."

Davis sighed. "Just because I didn't want him driving for my team any more doesn't mean I didn't like him as a person. I have been known to be able to separate personal and business on occasion."

"Since you normally mix the two, I assume it's okay to do it now."

"I don't see why not."

"Good. So, the real question is, who is on your radar right now? There are a ton of good drivers out there who won't have contracts at the end of the season."

"I'm very much aware of that. It's the ones without a contract on this circuit who interest me the most. I don't want some big team's leftover driver."

"Great minds think alike."

"And so do we—now, who are you thinking?"

"Based on our conversation three weeks ago, I thought that Fortson kid out of Ohio might be one to look at. He's young, has those devilishly good looks all the ladies love, and he's won six races on the Xfinity tour this season."

Davis took a deep breath. "Eh, I've seen him interviewed a few times. I don't think we'd get along."

"The pickings remain slim after that, in my opinion."

Davis heard footsteps outside the hauler. He stuck his head out the window but didn't see anything. "No, there's one driver I've wanted for a long time and this finally clears the way for me to hire him."

"Who's that?"

"J.T. Beaumont. If there's ever been a tailor-made driver for this team, it's him. We talked about it several months ago. I was just planting some seeds. Now it's time to pluck the fruit." He paused. "But there are a few other people we're going to have to get rid of first."

**

MOUTH AGAPE, CAL POKED his head out from underneath the Davis Motorsports hauler. He looked around and then scrambled to his feet. He checked over his shoulder before casually emerging from between the haulers. He was sure no one had seen him. He was also sure that the note shoved into his pocket wasn't a joke.

CHAPTER 4

OWEN BURNS ENJOYED his Monday morning commute to the Davis Motorsports headquarters in the quiet suburb of Huntersville. Thirty years ago, he left Clemson University with a master's degree in Mechanical Engineering, and a dream—to work in the auto racing industry. While his accomplishments stacked up, there was a glaring one missing. Not a single championship on his resume.

He'd come close several times, though he felt like winning a NASCAR championship was more a game of chance than skill. Mere hundredths of a second separated drivers on any given race day, but a bump here,,a wreck there, or an untimely start, and a good day's work could vanish.

Ah, who cares?

But Burns couldn't fool himself. He wanted to be able to say that he worked on a championship crew, yet he couldn't. And as he entered the twilight of his career, he wondered if he ever would. This season seemed like his best shot, and now, not only was his chance gone, but so was Tanner.

He pulled into the parking lot and lumbered toward the facility. The Davis Motorsports headquarters covered 65 sprawling acres in the North Carolina hills. More than sixty employees worked daily at the building, doing everything to ensure that the team had the best opportunity to win each week. From the outside, the grounds gave the appearance of a successful entity, one that triumphed over its competitors. In reality, it was a cash-strapped team that sought to gain every advantage when possible.

While other race teams had the cash to hire car chiefs and crew chiefs, Burns shouldered the burden of both jobs. He welcomed the challenge of managing the egos of crew members while still having a firm grip on how the car was running and what adjustments were required. Today would consist of a frank discussion about both.

As he entered the building, Burns heard the crew bickering at the end of the hall. He stopped and clenched his fists. He wanted to join them and blame somebody—or hit something. But he took a deep breath and walked into the room.

"Quiet," he said. "The last thing we need to do is start pointing fingers. Tanner's gone and it was an accident. Our thoughts should be with his wife and family, not over who might have made a mistake. Stuff happens. It's called racing."

Jackson Holmes stood up. "I agree. There's nothing good that comes out of blaming others. Everyone knows the risks when they climb into the car."

Russ Ross folded his arms and grunted. "No driver ever expects to have his throttle stuck wide open on a track like that in Texas."

"I swear that return spring on the throttle was perfect when I checked it," Dirt said.

"Of course you'd say that," Ross quipped. "It was your

responsibility to check."

Dirt stood up and bowed his chest. "Just what exactly are you implying?"

Ross rolled his eyes. "I think you know what I meant by that."

"Come over here and I'll knock your teeth—at least the ones you have left," Dirt growled.

Ross stood up before Burns slid in between the two men and held them off. "Gentlemen, have you forgotten what I said already?"

"Nobody's forgotten," Ross said. "We just don't believe this scum bag."

Dirt lunged at Ross but didn't make contact as Burns shoved him away.

"Look, we need to focus on getting a car set up for Phoenix and not trying to undo something that can't be undone," Burns said. "It's the part of our sport that nobody likes, but you can't avoid it sometimes. It just happens and you have to deal with it."

Ross and Dirt backed away from each other and returned to their seats on opposite sides of the room.

Before Burns could utter another word, Ned Davis walked into the room. "Do we have a problem, gentlemen?" he asked.

The crew members all shook their heads.

"This is hard on everyone, but we need to stick together in times like these," Davis said. "We're all sad over losing someone as incredible as Tanner, but you all still have a job to do. There's still a race on Sunday. There's still a crowd to entertain."

"Who do you plan on getting as Tanner's replacement?"

Ross asked.

"Just leave that up to me," Davis answered. "I'll find a driver that will get this team back in position to win it all again next season. Don't you worry."

"I'm not worried," Ross said. "I'm just wondering if you're going to be able to find any competent driver who's going to want to join a team where a crew member doesn't check the car sufficiently and may die as a result."

Dirt glared at Ross. "You wanna go right now? Right here? Cause I'm ready."

Davis put his hands in the air. "Gentlemen, please. Are you not listening to a word I'm saying? You're not irreplaceable, just remember that." Davis scanned the room. "Now, let's be a little bit more respectful of one another. You do your job and I'll do mine of finding us another driver who can win us a championship. Understand?"

The crew members nodded.

"Now that we've got that taken care of, let's get down to business," Burns said. "Anybody got any suggestions about how we can tweak the car for the race at Phoenix?"

Ross stood up. "Make sure the throttle doesn't get stuck." He glared at Dirt.

"It's on," Dirt said as he rushed Ross.

The two men grappled for a few moments before Ross threw Dirt to the ground and delivered a few punches. Dirt scrambled to his feet and lunged at Ross. Once Dirt grabbed him, their clash spilled in Holmes' direction. They tumbled toward Holmes, who tried to get out of the way but couldn't. Dirt jabbed at both men, landing punches to the face on both of them.

Burns sat back in his chair, arms folded.

Just get it out of your system, boys.

The trio tussled for another minute until they all stood up and resigned themselves to the fact that fighting wasn't going to change anything or get any answers.

"Are you three done?" Burns asked.

Dirt felt his bloodied lip with his index finger and stared at the blood. "Why I ought to—"

"You ought to what?" Ross asked. He checked his lip for blood, but there was nothing to be found. "Apologize?"

Dirt's eyes narrowed. "Don't you mock me. I'll take you out right now."

"Enough!" Burns shouted. "I thought I worked for Davis Motorsports with a bunch of adults, not a bunch of middle schoolers. Now, let's turn our attention to the task at hand—which is getting a car ready for Phoenix, no matter who's driving it."

The men settled into their chairs and stared at Burns.

"Well, does anyone have anything to say?" Burns asked. He scanned the room for any inkling that one of the men might want to speak, conciliatory or not.

"Maybe we can find someone who can drive worth a damn now," Dirt said.

CHAPTER 5

CAL'S PLANE BOUNCED and bumped on landing before rolling to its gate at the Charlotte airport. He glanced down at his hands, knuckles white after gripping the armrest for a nervous thirty seconds. It had been a while since terror like that had stricken him, though a bumpy landing seemed rather benign compared to having a gun pointed at his head. But at the moment, Cal considered the mundane direction in his life better suited for him now that he and his wife Kelly had a young daughter and a different lifestyle.

He spotted Kelly and Maddie as soon as he emerged from the secured terminal area. Maddie, who was just learning to talk, held up a sign: "Welcome home, Daddy!" Cal smiled and went for a group hug before he pried Maddie out of Kelly's arms and twirled her around.

Once they arrived at their car, Cal fastened Maddie into her car seat and got into the passenger's side. He leaned over and kissed Kelly as she cranked the engine.

Kelly cut her eyes toward him. "How many more weeks of this do we have with you being gone?"

He patted her on the leg. "The season's almost over, honey. Two more races and then life gets back to normal."

She let out a sigh. "I hope so. You being gone every

weekend is getting old."

***

LATER THAT AFTERNOON, Cal drove downtown for a meeting with his editor at the Observer office. He shook his head as he passed the Bank of America Stadium, home to the NFL's Carolina Panthers. Covering an NFL team meant eight short road trips per season. He'd already taken half that many trips in the past month and two more loomed on his schedule. Cal needed some assurances that this wasn't going to be a permanent move, as rumors on the staff began to circulate that Hal Thompson needed to retire for his health. Everyone knew it would kill Thompson to quit, but it would kill him if he didn't, according to his doctor.

But that wasn't the only thing Cal wanted to discuss. There was the more pressing matter of the note slipped into his pocket and Ned Davis' phone conversation that he overheard.

While Cal was new to the racing scene, he wasn't new to the idea that conspiracies are real. Over the years, he'd earned quite a reputation for being a conspiracy theorist. From the stock market to international politics to the NBA playoffs, he ascribed to more theories than most. Though he didn't mind the incessant teasing from his colleagues whenever a new theory emerged, Cal feared it hurt his chances of getting the green light to pursue sketchy happenings in the sports world. He'd have to handle his pitch to his editor with just the right aplomb or risk getting reduced to writing bland game stories and notebooks for the rest of the season. Like any other multi-million dollar enterprise, people who ran teams and had controlling interests didn't always play nice or fair.

Cal entered the building and walked by a somber Lisa Samuels, one of the advertising reps. A No. 39 flag adorned the side of her cubicle and she always wore a Carson Tanner t-shirt on casual Fridays during race season.

"You all right?" Cal asked.

She shrugged. "The good always die young, right?"

"Seems that way, doesn't it?"

"Well, it's not fair. Tanner was a great driver and an even better human being with his whole life in front of him. He could've broken every record given time. It's just so sad."

Cal nodded. "Hang in there, okay?"

Lisa put her head down and continued working.

While there were plenty of race fans around the office, no one seemed as shaken up about Tanner's death as Lisa— at least not as Cal walked through the building. However, the more die-hard race fans worked on the press, though most of them considered Carson Tanner too much of a pretty boy for their taste. They liked the rugged old timers, the drivers who didn't mind bumping another racer into the wall. Tanner wasn't one of those drivers, even though he'd banged a car or two out of the way when necessary. But it just wasn't enough to impress the long-time fans. Ever since Thompson's illness, the pressroom guys summoned Cal to break down all the weekend's action that he couldn't print or was cut from his story due to space limitations. Cal always wondered why they never seemed to read a word of his story. Their insatiable appetite for all things NASCAR made him realize why the paper spent so much money for him to fly around the country and watch drivers race circle a piece of asphalt 250 to 350 times, and write about it. Cal arrived at his desk fifteen minutes before the meeting with his editor, just so he could talk racing with the pressroom guys. He hustled downstairs where they were waiting for him.

"Quite a weekend of racin', Cal," Buster Farnum said. "It don't get any better than that."

"Yeah, unless you're not a fan of that jerk, Cashman," Gary Black said. "Burnin' out his tires while Tanner lay there dyin'. What a piece of trash."

Jody Phillips stood up. His 6-foot-4-inch frame cast a long shadow on the pressroom floor. "What'd you say about Cashman?"

Everyone stopped talking and turned toward Phillips. He glared at everyone on his crew.

Cal knew he was the only one present who could say something and not suffer repercussions later. "Settle down, Jody. We're just talking about the race. No need to get offended."

Jody grunted and sat back down.

"So, Cal, who's gonna take over for Tanner?" Buster said. "I heard it's gonna be Adelman—I love that guy."

Cal smiled. "And in what chat room did you hear that?"

"RubbinsRacin.com."

"I suggest you stay off that one," Cal quipped. "It's gonna be Beaumont."

"Beaumont?" Gary asked. "Are you kidding me?"

"You can post that one on your website chat room, just don't cite me as a source, okay?"

Buster nodded. "I can't believe that. I was sure it was gonna be Adelman."

"Nothing's for sure, but a little birdie told me that Beaumont is at the head of Ned Davis' short list."

"Well, I'll be," Gary said.

"Gotta run, guys, but I'll let you know something before it breaks," Cal said as he hustled toward the door.

***

WHEN CAL SETTLED into the chair in Marc Folsom's office, he received a directive that irked him.

"Good story on the race yesterday," Folsom said. "But I want you focused on racing, not off-the-track stuff this week. Got it?"

Cal leaned forward in his chair. "What do you mean? There's a ton of stuff happening that needs to be covered."

Folsom tapped his pen on his desk and stared at the television screen mounted in the corner of his office. "Thompson is on it."

"From his bed?"

Folsom looked at Cal, his eyes narrowing. "Yeah, from his bed. You got a problem with it?"

"No, I—"

"Thompson is the most connected writer on the NASCAR beat. If anything is happening, he knows about it. And I'd rather have him working on that stuff as opposed to you."

Cal sighed. "Well, there are two things we need to talk about."

"Shoot."

"First, your plans for next year with NASCAR coverage. I know you're using Thompson now, but I've heard he might be gone at the end of the year."

"You won't be on it—don't worry. I want to use your talents elsewhere, but this is where we are for now. What's the second thing?"

"I'm not sure what you're going to think about it now based on how you opened our conversation."

"Oh? And why's that?"

"It's because I've come upon some reliable information regarding the direction of Davis Motorsports' next target."

"Is that all? Because I don't mind letting you write about it."

"No. I also have reason to believe that Carson Tanner's death was no accident."

Folsom looked down and propped his forehead up with his hand. He closed his eyes while he spoke. "Cal, why must you be an insufferable conspiracy theorist? His throttle was clearly stuck and he slammed into the wall. End of story. There's nothing else to it."

"That's what somebody wanted you to think."

"And you know this how?"

Cal took a deep breath and reached into his pocket and pulled out the note. "Someone slipped this into my pocket yesterday after the crash." He handed the piece of paper to Folsom.

Folsom cracked a grin. "*That crash was no accident*—that's your big tip?"

"No, there's more. I was outside the Davis Motorsports team hauler after the race and I heard Ned Davis on the phone talking about how now that Tanner was out of the way, he could pursue Beaumont to take his place."

"Beaumont? Of all the driver's he'd take Beaumont?"

"You're not listening if you think that's the most important part of that conversation. Hello? What about 'now that Tanner is out of the way'? Doesn't that concern you?"

Folsom grunted and glanced back up at the television screen behind Cal. "You'll concoct a story out of anything, won't you?"

Cal leaned back in his chair. "I haven't concocted anything. Just start looking at the facts."

"The facts is, NASCAR is investigating the accident, and until they release anything contrary to what obviously happened—a stuck throttle—then there's no need to write such nonsense. Am I clear?"

"Yeah, but I think you're making a mistake. This is big news."

"It's big news if it's true. I doubt it is. Somebody was just messing with you. Maybe another writer trying to make you look stupid."

Cal stood up to leave. Folsom handed him the slip of paper and Cal slid it back into his jacket pocket. He pulled out his phone, which buzzed to let him know he'd received a direct message from his Twitter account.

"What is it now?" Folsom asked as Cal buried his face in his phone.

"I got a message from some follower."

"Another clue for you, Sherlock?"

Cal rolled his eyes. "No, but it's making me question everything." He turned the phone's screen toward Folsom. It read:

I know who did it

CHAPTER 6

TODD CASHMAN PUNCHED the button on the speakerphone and propped his feet up on the conference room table. He braced himself for the onslaught of questions about his victory celebration in Texas while a fellow driver was dead a few hundred yards away. He had no idea Carson Tanner was dead after slamming into the wall. And it was the truth.

But Cashman didn't care whether Tanner was alive or dead. Making the finals of the championship chase was all that mattered to him. He'd let the journalists parse out the details. He was going to run wide open in Phoenix without any fear of the consequences, since he'd already qualified for the final four.

"You ready, Todd?" asked the NASCAR media relations director.

"Let 'em fire away," he answered.

Fire away, they did.

"Harold Bailey from ESPN. What did you see from your perspective on that final lap in regards to Carson Tanner?" asked the first journalist.

"I saw Tanner fly into the wall."

"Any thought of slowing down?"

"This is racin', man. I never think about slowing down unless the caution is out or I'm told to pit my car."

Another journalist chimed in. "Gerald Stockton from Fox Sports. How bad did you think Tanner's crash was?"

"It looked bad, but I've seen worse and watched guys walk away from it. I figured he would've been fine."

"Shelton Bingham from Speed51.com. Do you have any regrets about your post-race celebration?"

Cashman sighed. "Not at all. We battle hard every week—and to be in this position at this point in the season is worth celebrating. Had I known Tanner was dead, maybe I would've toned it down a bit. But how was I to know. Besides, that's karma for you."

"Bailey here again. What exactly do you mean by 'that's karma'?"

"Come on, Bailey. You saw the race in Martinsville. Tanner put me into the wall and caused a massive wreck. He's always drove reckless and I'm not surprised that it's what also got him killed. I mean, I feel bad that it happened and really bad for his family, but if you race like he did, you've got to expect that something like that is going to eventually happen."

The line went silent. Cashman wondered if his connection remained live.

"Hello? Is anybody there?"

"The conference call is still in progress," the NASCAR official said. "Any more questions?"

Cashman fielded a handful of questions about what his approach would be to the race in Phoenix. He also answered some questions about his state of mind going into the race, knowing that one of his peers just died. They weren't the kind of questions he wanted to be answering. This was Cashman's moment in the sun and Carson Tanner was still casting a dark shadow over him even after his death.

When the fifteen-minute session ended, Cashman hung up and yelled for Brooke Wyatt, his media relations director.

"What was that all about?" Cashman demanded once he found her.

"What was what all about?" she asked.

"Those questions. Weren't you listening?"

She nodded. "You weren't expecting anybody to ask you about Tanner's death?"

"Well, no, maybe like a question or two, but not practically the entire time. I felt like they were giving me the fifth degree."

Staring down at her iPad, she cut her eyes at him. "Maybe you shouldn't have mentioned how his death was karma. Maybe you could've been a little gracious." She paused and wondered if she should continue before casting aside better judgment. "Maybe you shouldn't have acted like an insensitive jerk—and maybe they would've left you alone."

Cashman puffed his chest out. "Maybe you shouldn't talk to me like that any more. You are aware of what happened to my last media relations director, right? They didn't tell you that story?"

"I'm not sure I would've believed it, even if you told it to me yourself.'"

He stooped down and glared at her, eye to eye. "She had a smart mouth, so I fired her."

She appeared unflappable, ignoring his threats. "Much better than having a dumb mouth, like yours. If you think it was bad before, just wait until word of this press conference circulates. You're going to be public enemy number one."

Cashman grunted and looked down at his phone. "Enough of this nonsense." He stopped and shook his index finger at Brooke. "Don't ever let me get caught like this again. It's not cool. Not for the team or our sponsors. You got it?"

She gave him a half-hearted nod.

"Good. Now, let's get back to work."

***

AT THE DAVIS MOTORSPORTS HEADQUARTERS, the crew members shuffled into the meeting room and bantered about who made it home first.

"Did you get my text?" Holmes said. "12:04 in my driveway last night."

"That's because you only live thirty minutes from the airport," Ross said.

"I can't remember. We were playing miles-per-hour rules or first one home?" Dirt asked.

"If it was miles per hour, I would've won," Burns said.

"We were playing first one home—period," Holmes snipped.

Ross didn't miss a beat. "Said the guy who made it home first."

Burns waved everybody off. "It doesn't matter, to be honest. What matters is that we get our car ready for whoever is going to drive it on Sunday."

"I can't even believe Davis is going to try to get someone to drive the 39 car this week," Holmes said.

"The show must go on," Burns said. "But there's something we need to do first."

"Which is?" Dirt asked.

"Listen to Cashman's conference call. I wanna hear what he has to say." Burns surfed to the website and cranked up the volume.

Twenty minutes later once the interview was over, Ross stood up and slammed the laptop closed in disgust.

"Can you believe that guy?" Dirt asked.

"Yeah," Ross said. "If he didn't say junk like that, I'd think it was an impostor on the line."

"Well, I never wish ill-will on anyone, but I'll make an exception for Cashman. I really hope his car bursts into flames on the first lap. It'd serve him right for those comments. Besides, anyone with a pair of good eyes knows that Tanner never touched him in Martinsville. Cashman went into the wall all by himself. I can't believe he's still peddling the idea that Tanner bumped him."

"Let him hang himself," Ross said.

Holmes remained quiet, content to type away on his phone to his sizeable Twitter followers irate over Cashman's comments.

"What'd you think, Holmes? You're not saying a word," Dirt said.

"Leave him be," Ross said. "He's having woman problems."

"Well, we all need our heads in the game this week," Dirt snapped. "Woman problems or not. We need to do whatever we can to get this car running like a dream for whoever takes it over."

Holmes broke his silence. "I heard it was going to be

Beaumont."

"Seriously? We got no chance now."

"Who cares if we win or not this week," Holmes said. "It doesn't matter any more. We're out of the chase."

"It matters to me," Dirt said. "I want to prove to someone out there that I'm the best there is—and even if there's a driver change mid-season, I can still get a car in shape to win a race."

Holmes rolled his eyes. "You really think any of this is all about you?"

Dirt sat up straight and glared at Holmes. "Dang straight, it is. The best driver in the world ain't gonna win a soapbox derby without a fast machine."

"True. But nobody cares about what we do on Sunday. It's just window dressing at this point," Holmes said.

Ross scanned the room, staring at his fellow crew members. He turned his attention toward Dirt. "What I really can't believe is that you ever used to work for that scumbag Cashman."

Dirt shrugged. "You do whatever you can to break in. I can't say I'm proud of it, but it is what it is. You would've done the same, given the opportunity."

Ross grunted. "I doubt it. I've always hated that SOB."

"Now, gentlemen, is this anyway to start our Tuesday morning?" Holmes said.

Dirt grunted. He glanced back down at his phone and began to type a message.

"Whatcha doin' there, Dirt?" Ross asked.

"Just buzz off, man. I'm not in the mood this morning," Dirt said. His fingers flew furiously on his cell phone. He pounded out his message: It won't be long now.

CHAPTER 7

JESSICA TANNER EASED onto the examination table while her doctor waited. She was well past the first trimester, which had taken its toll on her, and over halfway past her second. Her body had been handling all the changes just fine up until Tanner's death. If she could've just locked herself in her house and curled up in a corner, that's what she would've done. But her connection to her husband remained alive through the little baby growing in her womb. It was the one thing in her life that kept her from losing all hope amidst the insanity.

"How have you been feeling?" Dr. Margaret Woodland asked. "Any changes you think you need to tell me about?" She poked around Jessica's belly.

"Not really. I mean, I've never been pregnant before, so I don't exactly know what normal is. If you mean, am I still craving ice cream? Yes. But that was no different than before, to be honest with you."

The doctor shared a laugh with Jessica as she continued the examination. "I'm glad to hear that," she said before she stopped. She backed away from Jessica and made some notes on her chart. "You can put your shirt down now."

Jessica sat up. "So, is everything all right?"

"Well, your most recent blood work has shown some slight irregularities and I want us to take a closer look at the baby."

"What do you mean?"

"There's a screening procedure we can do to test to see if there are any abnormalities with your daughter."

"What kind of procedure?"

"There's several actually. One is an echocardiogram. But there's also a more invasive one. Have you ever heard of amniocentesis?"

Jessica shook her head. "No, should I?"

"Since this is your first pregnancy, probably not. It's a test we use to determine if your baby might have genetic defects. We just want to make sure everything is okay, or if we need to take a more invasive approach to correct any abnormalities."

"What do you think is wrong?"

"Well, it's too early to tell at this point if it's serious or not, but I think there may be some problems with the baby's heart."

"Fine," Jessica said. "Let's do it. Do them all. I want to do whatever I can to help this little girl."

***

LATER THAT AFTERNOON, Jessica awoke from her nap when the phone buzzed. It was Dr. Woodland.

"Jessica, I'd like to schedule a follow-up with you tomorrow, if you can make it at all," Dr. Woodland said. "I know you're going through a tough time and have a lot going on, but this is important."

Jessica sat up. "What is it, doc? Is there something wrong."

"Now, these tests aren't a hundred percent accurate, but we found some of those abnormalities I was afraid of."

"What does that mean?"

"For now, it means that we need to keep a closer eye on your baby's development."

"Don't beat around the bush. Does she have Down's Syndrome?"

Dr. Woodland sighed. "No, but your baby does have a congenital heart defect."

"What does that mean?"

"We need to do some more tests, but based on my early prognosis, I think we might need to perform an open fetal surgery. It's that severe."

Jessica dropped the phone and wailed.

No! How could this be happening to me?

She started to hyperventilate.

Breathe, Jessica. Breathe.

She stood up and started to pace around the house.

It's okay. You've had bad stuff happen in your life before. You can do this.

She walked into the kitchen and began to slice an apple for a snack. She was less interested in eating a piece of fruit than she was in relieving the tension she felt welling up within her. As she concluded her nervous culinary habit, she jammed the tip of the knife into the cutting board.

"I can't do this," she cried aloud as she crumpled to the floor.

Snap out of it, Jessica. You can do this. Just pull it together.

She stood up, brushed her blouse off, and strode toward

the living room to retrieve her phone. Just as she was about to dial her mother's number, she noticed she had a voicemail.

"Hi, Mrs. Tanner. This is Stewart Paxton from National Insurance. We need to talk with you pronto."

Jessica took down his number and dialed it.

"Mr. Paxton? This is Jessica Tanner. You left me a message."

"Yes, Mrs. Tanner. Thank you so much for calling me back. I'm really sorry for your loss."

"Thanks."

"I'm afraid I'm calling with a bit of bad news, which I know isn't what you want to hear at this time, but I wanted to let you know now so you could plan accordingly."

"What kind of bad news?"

"Your husband's coverage only dealt with death or illness that happened to something unrelated to his racing."

"What are you trying to say?"

"I'm saying that if he died in a car accident on the way home from the airport, he would be covered."

Jessica grabbed a tuft of hair with her free hand and pulled. "So, he's not covered?"

"That's correct, ma'am. We're going to have to deny this claim."

Jessica's breathing became short. "What do you mean, you're denying this claim? I'm not going to get anything?"

"I'm really sorry, but that's the case here. His policy covered hardly anything that happened on the race track."

"Hardly? So, there's something that it did cover?"

"In the very rare and off chance that someone intentionally and willfully attempted to end your husband's life on the race track, then, yes, the policy will be paid out. That'd fall under the murder clause. But NASCAR released their findings to us this morning and they determined it to be a faulty part that caused the accident. Unfortunately, that's not covered."

"You have to be kidding me? This is crazy. I'm pregnant! And my baby needs an expensive surgery!"

"Again, Mrs. Tanner, I'm sorry for your loss and I wish there was better news or more I could do for you, but at this time, that's it."

"You better believe you're gonna hear from my lawyer," she snapped before slamming the phone down.

She crumpled to the floor, an even bigger mess now than she was five minutes ago. Without giving it a second thought, she wiped her nose with her sleeve and stood up. She stumbled back toward her bedroom where Carson had left her with a contact list of people to call in case something ever happened to him.

"Where is that number?" she said as she scanned the list. Her finger finally fell on it. "Ah-ha."

She punched in the numbers on her cell phone and waited.

"This is Eddie Simpson."

Jessica cleared her throat before speaking. "Hi, Mr. Simpson. This is Jessica Tanner."

"Oh, Mrs. Tanner. I'm so sorry for your loss."

"Thank you. I appreciate that."

"If there's anything we can do for you here, please let us know. We'd love to help."

"Well, in that case, can you please release a statement saying that Carson's accident was no accident?"

"I'm not sure I'm following you."

"I just got a call from my insurance company telling me that they are denying my claim for Carson's life insurance policy payout because the accident was just that—an accident. If someone willfully tried to put him into the wall, they would've paid out. But because Carson was cheap and bought a crumby life insurance policy, I'm stuck."

Simpson let out a long moan. "Oh, Jessica. I'm so sorry. I wish we could do something about that, but I'm afraid we can't. Our investigators have already wrapped up their inquiry into the matter and we just found it to be a faulty part."

"There has to be something else you can do," she insisted. "Surely there's some bereavement fund or assistance for the family of lost drivers."

"Right about now, I wish we'd started one. But that's simply not the case. At this point, we can't do much—and while I want to help you, I can't falsify any documents just so you can receive a life insurance policy payout."

Jessica stamped her foot. "All this talk about NASCAR being a family is bull. What kind of family ignores the loved ones of a lost driver?"

"I understand you're upset, Mrs. Tanner, but the facts are what the facts are. It doesn't make it any less tragic, but it's what happened. And I—"

Jessica didn't wait to hear the rest of his rant. She was done. Done with all of it. She wished she could just stay in her room and drown her sorrows in bowls of ice cream— or alcohol.

After a few moments, she took several deep breaths and regained her composure.

Then she felt her baby kick again—and another wave of sorrow rolled over her.

CHAPTER 8

RON PARKER STARED at the desert, his scenery out of the front of his RV windshield for the past ten hours. But a scene from a few days before that lasted all of ten seconds dominated his thoughts. He knew what he saw, yet he had no idea how to proceed.

He looked over at his wife, Nancy, who slumbered in the passenger seat. To him, she deserved sainthood. *I picked a good one.* Not many women would embrace his obsession with NASCAR and spend their early retirement years driving from track to track every weekend. Parker installed appliances for a major home improvement store for nearly 35 years before he retired. His life had been anything but a dream, but he felt like he was living in one now—almost.

If Parker had his druthers, he would have owned a car and spent years on the NASCAR circuit as a famous driver. He'd experienced some mild success racing sprint cars on dirt tracks in the Midwest, but when a blood clot led to a minor stroke in his early twenties, it dashed any hopes he had of making a career out of it. With his right leg partially paralyzed, there was no way he could have handled the demands of competitive racing.

He looked down at his speedometer, holding steady at 70.

Thank God for cruise control.

This was the second year Parker had signed up to help the Davis Motorsports Team sell memorabilia at the different tracks. But ever the work-a-holic, he also covered security shifts for sick or absent volunteers. He and his wife followed the tour and went to work a couple of days before the race, selling merchandise to fans or guarding a chain-link gate. It wasn't much money, but it was enough to cover gas and food. However, monetary gain was near the bottom on his list of reasons to sign up for such menial tasks. There was another motivation at the very top, one he never mentioned to Nancy.

The reasons Parker proffered to her centered around his desire to gain access the pits and get to know the drivers. He sold the idea well. He and Nancy decided that they would spend each week getting to know a different driver. Sometimes they would introduce themselves and end up spending thirty minutes or more engaged in a conversation with a driver. Other times, it'd be nothing more than a quick pose for a picture. Then there were the crew members, the backstage magicians who made sure the drivers had the best chance to win each week. And they got to know them too.

That's why Parker knew something was awry the second he glanced at the No. 39 car in the garage at the Texas Motor Speedway. The garage area remained quiet until it opened at 7 o'clock the morning of the race. But someone had snuck in there and was doing something they shouldn't have been—at least in Parker's estimation. He only saw it all by chance when he couldn't sleep and climbed atop his RV to watch the sun rise.

After two years of being close to the action on the circuit, he knew such activity was rare. In fact, during that time he'd never seen anybody working on a car before the garage was open. And he dismissed it as no big deal and forgot about it—until he watched Carson Tanner's No. 39 car careen into the wall on the final lap and skid to a stop in a crumpled heap of metal. He was convinced it was no accident.

But what to do? He had no proof of what he'd seen. Investigators ruled it an accident. Everyone seemed to move on. It's racing. Sometimes drivers crash—and sometimes they die. Maybe there wasn't anything to do. Regardless of how the racing world moved forward so quickly, Parker wanted to linger on it. He needed to, for he saw a way to make all his problems disappear, perhaps even have a normal retirement. After all, he wasn't sure he could fabricate another reason why they needed to continue following the circuit. The real one sickened him.

With Nancy still sound asleep, Parker scanned the radio dial for something to pass the time. He found a station broadcasting his favorite conservative talk show host. Parker chuckled as the man lampooned congress; a recent poll showed them as being only two percentage points more favorable with the U.S. public than the latest Middle Eastern terrorist group blowing up American interests overseas. The host then went to break and a news segment started.

Authorities in Nevada today are searching for Bill Goldini in connection with a brazen murder at a casino in Las Vegas on Saturday. Goldini, who has spent time in prison after a racketeering conviction along with his father Jim Goldini, is rumored to be the heir-apparent to the Goldini crime syndicate. Officials say …

Parker turned the radio off in disgust and stared out the window.

What's this world coming to?

He preferred not to dwell on such things too long. Life was too short to spend it worrying about all the crazy people in the world.

He looked up and noticed the Arizona state border sign, signaling that their long journey would soon be over—another week safe from his demons. At least, that's what he hoped.

Nancy twisted in her seat and squinted as she stared at her husband.

"Where are we?"

"Good afternoon, little angel. Someone got a good nap." He pointed at her shirt, which appeared damp from drool.

She grabbed a tissue and blotted it. "Oh, cut it out, Ron."

He snickered and turned his attention back to the road. "We just entered Arizona. Got about five more hours left until we get to Phoenix."

"Avondale, honey, we're going to Avondale."

He shook his head and rolled his eyes. Nancy remained a stickler when it came to talking about the precise location of a track. It drove Parker nuts. Every time someone asked them where they were from, he'd answer, "Columbus, Ohio." She'd punch his arm and say, "We don't live in Columbus. We live in Powell." Unless the person was from the Columbus area, Parker saw nothing but blank stares until he'd clarify. "Powell is a suburb of Columbus," he'd say, which would be met by a knowing head bob. He used to tell her to stop that practice, but he quit trying after twenty years of marriage. Nancy didn't have that many faults, and he decided it was best to let it go and just explain where Powell was.

Parker's phone buzzed and Nancy snatched it off the console.

"Hey," Parker said. "Gimme that."

"Who's calling you? I wonder." She punched in the code for his phone and didn't see a missed call but a photo texted to him. She gasped and held it up for him to see. "What's this all about?"

Parker stayed calm. "Oh, it's probably just one of the guys having fun."

"Having fun? Pointing a gun at the camera, taking a picture, and then sending you a message that says, 'Time's up.' That's having fun?"

"You know how Larry is," Parker said as he reached for the phone.

"Honey, that wasn't from Larry."

"Oh?" he said as he scrolled to his texts.

She playfully hit his hand. "Stop texting and driving."

He put the phone down. "Then who was it from?"

"Some guy named Butch. Now, I don't know much, but when a guy named Butch takes a picture of himself brandishing a gun and adds, 'Time's up,' I take that seriously."

Parker laughed. "I don't know anybody named Butch. Someone must have typed in my number by mistake. No worries."

He waited until she was looking out of her window before he grabbed his phone again. He deleted the photo and slid the phone back onto the console.

"Some psycho killer would accidentally start texting you, wouldn't he?" she added as she turned her gaze back toward him. "I hope he doesn't think you're really the person he's after and is tracking you by using your phone."

"Me, too," he said as he reached for his phone and turned it off. "Me, too."

She turned back over and went to sleep.

Parker waited for a few minutes to make sure she was actually asleep instead of attempting to take a nap. When he was satisfied that she was asleep, he rolled his window down and glanced at the mile marker.

Mile number 303.

Then he flung the phone out of the window.

CHAPTER 9

CAL WOKE UP WEDNESDAY with a feeling that something wasn't right. Call it instinct. Call it intuition. He didn't care. He simply knew that something about Tanner's accident—one he played over and over in his mind—wasn't a freak event. It felt planned, if not perfectly timed. The idea had already gripped him that something else was at play that day, and he wasn't ready to relinquish it.

"Are you all right, honey?" Kelly asked.

Cal rubbed his face. "Sure. Why?"

"You were awfully restless last night. I don't know what was going on with you, but I wouldn't have wanted to be in those dreams."

"Did I say anything?"

She rolled over and gazed at him. "Not that I could make out. It was mostly gibberish." She paused, looking him up and down before continuing. "I have no idea how coherent you were, but I didn't understand any of it. Whatever it was, though, you sounded stressed out, paranoid even."

"When am I not paranoid?" he shot back.

"Good point. It carries over from your waking hours to your sleeping habits. Lucky me."

Cal leaned over and kissed her before climbing out of

bed. "You're an angel."

She smirked at him before turning over and closing her eyes.

Cal got dressed and ate his breakfast, poring over a copy of the *Charlotte Observer*. It was a morning ritual that never escaped him when he was home.

He read a story about a man named Franklin Guyton who was wrongly imprisoned for twenty-five years before forensic evidence proved him innocent.

A quote from the article jumped off the page at him: "Sometimes the most obvious answers aren't the right ones," said Mecklenburg District Attorney Ashton Myers. "We all worked under the assumption that Mr. Guyton was guilty based on the standard of a preponderance of evidence, not the standard of beyond a reasonable doubt. I'm happy to say that today the courts got this case right and reversed its course in overturning the conviction of Mr. Guyton."

It was the first phrase that ate at Cal: "Sometimes the most obvious answers aren't the right ones."

For the NASCAR world, the obvious answer regarding Carson Tanner's death was that it was an accident. His throttle got stuck and he struck the wall with such force that it killed him. That's what it looked like anyway. Who would ever suspect anything different? After all, everyone who attends races—from the drivers all the way down to the six-year-old boy sitting on the front row—knows the inherent danger of zipping around a track at over a hundred miles per hour.

Yet somebody—or maybe more than just one somebody—was trying to tell Cal that the obvious answer wasn't the right one.

He then picked up his phone and dialed Max Folsom's number.

"Geez, Cal, it's nine o'clock. Don't you ever sleep?" Folsom griped.

"Sorry, boss. I didn't work until one a.m. putting the paper to bed."

"Put a little thought into it, okay?"

"Fine. I'll call you back later."

"No, no," Folsom protested. "I'm already up. I might as well hear what this is all about—and it better be good."

Cal took a deep breath. "Here's the thing. I just can't get it out of my head that maybe Tanner's accident was anything but that."

"Here we go again."

"Please, hear me out," Cal snapped. "Now, I went back and did some research on his old races last night and couldn't find a single incident of him wrecking on his own."

Folsom grunted. "There's a first time for everything."

"Sure, but he could've driven backward across the finish line and won the race on Sunday. Why risk it?"

Folsom sighed. "He didn't, Cal. That's why it's called an accident. Get it?"

"No, I understand that. But something just doesn't seem right about it all."

"Why? Because someone slipped you a note?"

"And then sent me a message on Twitter. Someone is trying to tell me something."

"I'm trying to tell you something too, so listen closely," Folsom said. "Let it go. It was an accident."

"For the record, I don't like this."

"Cal, based on your track record, I don't think you've

ever met a conspiracy theory that you didn't like."

Cal seethed. "I think the hunches I pursue speak for themselves. I've got a shelf lined with awards if you'd like to see them."

"And you haven't won an award since you've been here," Folsom countered. "You know I like you, Cal, but you've got to stop with all this. It's going to reflect poorly on the paper as well as impact your credibility as a journalist. Please don't try to write anything to this effect or even put it out through one of your social media channels. Please, Cal. I'm begging you to stop with this fool's errand."

Cal banged his fist on the counter. "Fine. I won't write anything about it. But I'm going to keep digging and I'm going to come back with something that you'd be a fool not to print."

"Until that moment comes, don't overstep your bounds. Got it?"

"Yeah, yeah. I got it."

Cal hung up and tossed his phone onto the counter with disgust.

Kelly shuffled into the kitchen, bouncing Maddie on her hip. She rubbed his back with her free hand and kissed him on the cheek.

"What's wrong now?" she asked. "You feel a little tense."

He waved dismissively. "It's just Folsom being Folsom. He and I don't see eye-to-eye on this potentially explosive story about Carson Tanner."

Her eyes widened. "Did something else come out about the accident?"

"No, but I did my own research and none of it makes sense."

"Didn't his throttle get stuck?"

"Yeah, but I got this note." He pulled it out of his pocket and showed it to her.

She read it aloud: "That crash was no accident."

Then he handed her his cell phone with the message on it: "I know who did it."

"Somebody's probably just messing with you, honey."

"If so, they're doing a pretty darn good job. But between these notes and Tanner's history as a driver, I think maybe foul play might be involved."

Kelly cocked her head as the corners of her mouth turned upward. "Don't you almost always suspect foul play whenever an athlete dies?"

Cal chuckled. "Guilty as charged—but that's only because a lot of times it is."

She grabbed his hands. "Well, this isn't one of the usual sports you cover. I remember drivers dying in wrecks on the track in the past. Maybe that's just what happened."

"But it's been a while due to safety precautions." He paused. "I don't know. It just seems really odd to me the way it went down."

"Just think about it, Cal. It's the last lap of a race and he runs into a wall. Do you really think anyone could plan that?"

He shook his head. "Someone could have planned to sabotage his car and it just happened when it happened."

"But on the last lap when he has to win to qualify for the championship?"

Cal stopped. "I didn't realize you were such a race fan."

She kissed him on the cheek again and smiled. "You know I read everything you write. I know it's far more interesting to talk about when you get home rather than discussing how many times Maddie pooped in her pants the day before."

He reached up and pinched Maddie's bulging cheeks. "Awww, don't say that. I want to know *everything* that happens to Maddie—except her bowel movements."

She laughed and shook her head. "Are you ready for your flight to Phoenix today?"

"Almost. Got a few things I need to do at the office before I head to the airport."

"Well, I'm gonna miss you at the gun range today."

"I'm gonna miss it, too. It's been good for me."

She smiled. "To let out all that pent up frustration you have from all those people calling you a hack in the comments section of your article."

"It's a good way to let off some steam." Cal's phone buzzed. "Excuse me for a moment," he said as he got up and walked toward the living room.

"This is Cal."

The voice on the other line sounded hysterical. "Mr. Murphy, this is Jessica Tanner, Carson's wife. I was wondering if you could help me before I lose my mind."

"Just calm down," he said. "Take a deep breath and talk to me—and I'll see if I can help you. What's going on?"

"Carson's insurance company isn't going to pay out the policy because it was limited to accidents off the track, not accidents on it."

"I understand. There's not much I can do about that."

"Well, the policy does cover something that isn't an accident on the track."

"You mean, like if someone intentionally try to hurt him?"

"Exactly."

"Not to be insensitive or anything, but nobody hit him when he ran into that wall."

"Everybody knows that—but that's not what I'm talking about. I'm talking about someone tinkering with his car to make it crash."

Cal's eyebrows shot upward. "To be honest, I've been wondering how he could just crash on the final lap like that. It's not like he needed to run wide open to win the race."

"Maybe the throttle did get stuck, but maybe it didn't."

"Is there anything you're going to do about it?"

"I'm launching an independent investigation. I'd love for you to follow it, maybe even help me put pressure on the insurance company."

Cal took a deep breath. "Look, Mrs. Tanner. I'm happy to help you in a way that's appropriate for me as a journalist. But I can't write something just to put pressure on an insurance company. That's not what I do."

She started crying softly. "I just don't know how I'm going to do it."

"Do what?"

"Take care of this baby, that's what. We hardly have any money as Tanner wasn't making that much yet—and almost everything he made was going to pay off some massive debt he'd accrued before we got married."

"I'm sorry to hear that."

"And to make matters worse, I just found out that our little girl has a congenital heart defect."

"Aww, Mrs. Tanner, I'm so sorry to hear that."

She blew her nose near her phone's receiver, startling Cal. "If you think that my husband was murdered out there on the track, don't you shy away from writing about it. It's going to be hard enough raising this little girl full time, much less make ends meet."

Cal almost told her about the messages, then he stopped. Now wasn't the time. But if her independent investigation of the crash found something else, he wouldn't just tell her—he'd tell the world.

CHAPTER 10

THE SUN CREPT OVER the Arizona hills, and Ned Davis was already perched atop his RV. He didn't care that his team's car had yet to arrive at the Phoenix International Raceway; it didn't stop him from getting up early to watch the practice runs of the lowly K&N West Series cars. If anyone recognized him there, they might accuse him of scouting for a new driver. But he already had his man. His presence had less to do with trying to replace Carson Tanner and more to do with his love for the sport.

Nothing like the smell of fuel and burnt rubber in the morning. Beats coffee any day of the week.

Davis watched the cars fly around the track. He stared down at a sheet of paper that listed all the cars trying to qualify for the race later that evening.

With NASCAR imposed limitations that kept the lower level circuit cars from running as fast, David ignored the overall times and watched how the drivers handled the oddly shaped track that once was a road course. A driver who understood how to hold his line was a driver that was destined to succeed.

Davis put a tick by Austin Andrews' name, as he drove with precision. He didn't have to check the times to know that Andrews was the fastest driver so far.

Perhaps if Beaumont doesn't work out …

A loud rapping on the side of his RV startled Davis. He glanced down from atop his RV to recognize *Observer* reporter Cal Murphy.

He leaned over the side. "Well, if it isn't the great Cal Murphy."

Cal nodded. "You're too kind, Mr. Davis."

"Call me Ned," he said as he climbed down.

Cal continued. "Besides, you must not read the comments below my stories posted on the Internet. I can assure you no one there is calling me great."

Davis laughed. "I never read that stuff. It's just a waste of time." He finished climbing down the ladder and jumped off the last step, landing flat-footed. "So, what do you want to talk about today?"

Cal looked down. "Not happy stuff I'm afraid. I wanna talk about Carson Tanner."

"I expected as much."

"I'm actually surprised to see you here."

Davis shook his head. "I don't mourn well. I hate funerals. The only one I'd go to might be my wife's—if I actually have one who dies first. Most of them can't wait for me to die and just try to take all my money now." He laughed and slapped Cal on the arm. "Know what I mean?"

"Must be a tough life."

"It is, especially when you're as rich as I am and you're trying to figure out who genuinely cares about you and who's just after your money."

"I wouldn't know anything about that."

Davis chuckled. "Good. More money, more problems. That's what I say. But I'm not interested in going back, if you know what I'm sayin'. They're mostly good problems to have—mostly."

"We all have our problems," Cal said.

"Yes, we do. And one of yours is probably a deadline. So, let's step inside here." Davis motioned for Cal to proceed into the hauler.

Once inside, Davis led Cal through the narrow passageway leading to the largest meeting space on the truck. It was just large enough for a couple of couches, which surrounded the perimeter. Cal took a seat on one side and Davis settled in opposite him.

Davis dug a can of smokeless tobacco out of his back pocket and jammed a pinch of it between his lip and gum. He brushed his hands together and picked up a cup to spit into. "So, what do you wanna know about Carson Tanner?"

Cal shifted in his seat. "I guess my initial comment was misleading. I know plenty about Tanner. I'm interested in some other information."

Davis spewed a stream of tobacco juice into his cup and cocked his head to the side. "Such as?"

"Did Carson Tanner have any enemies that you know of?"

Davis chuckled. "Well, this certainly isn't the direction I thought you'd take for our interview. And to be honest, for a reporter who claims to know plenty about him, that seems like an absurd question."

"Nevertheless, it begs to be answered."

Davis sighed and shook his head. "Why do you guys have to dig up dirt on a dead man?"

"With all due respect, sir, I'm not trying to dig up dirt on Tanner. I'm merely trying to put to rest the idea that this was actually murder instead of an accident."

Davis grunted and sat up straight. "Murder? What kind of cockamamie idea is that? Carson Tanner died in an accident on the track. It's unfortunate, but it was in plain sight. Who'd even dare to suggest such a thing?"

Cal nodded. "I tend to agree with you, but I have a source that insinuated the accident wasn't an accident at all, but a targeted attack."

"Even if it was, how could anyone sabotage a car so dramatically? It's impossible."

"Maybe it was just good timing."

"Bull. There was nothing about that accident that looked suspicious. Anyone who's been around the sport very long knows what a stuck throttle looks like. It ain't pretty when it happens, but we've all seen the footage of when it's happened to drivers in the past. Thankfully, it hasn't happened that often, but it's unmistakable when it does."

"Perhaps that was the point."

Davis spit into his cup and leaned back. "You risk credibility when you levy accusations like this, Mr. Murphy. Nobody is going to believe you."

"What if NASCAR learns something different?"

"They won't because it was an accident. They'll conclude what you already know deep down—that it was an accident." He paused for a moment. "You ought to be ashamed of yourself for trying to create some scandalous story just to get more eyeballs on your article."

"I assure you, Mr. Davis, my creativity does not extend to fabricating stories. I don't deal well in the fiction genre. I stick to facts and evidence and corroboration from witnesses. I have two out of the three so far and it's only a matter of time before the evidence I need will surface."

Davis rubbed his face with one of his hands, closing his eyes as he did. He shook his head. "Mr. Murphy, you live in a different world from the rest of us. People in this world want to read about what you know for sure, not about what you think happened."

"I'm sorry that I can't share with you everything I know, but I often trust my gut in these situations—and my gut is telling me that my cockamamie theory is dead on."

"I admire your tenacity—I truly do. But you're missing it on this one. And this isn't the kind of story you want to miss it on."

"Why? Because someone died?"

"No. It's because of the people who are still living. Carson Tanner was beloved by all and he died in a tragic accident on the track. Everybody knows it. It's not worth ruining your career over because you have a hunch about something. Just think about it."

Cal nodded. "I have thought about it—which is exactly why I think I need to pursue this story more. Something happened out there far beyond a simple stuck throttle. That throttle got some help. And if you're not going to assist me in finding out who did this, I have my ways of figuring it out myself."

"Enter at your own risk, Mr. Murphy."

Cal stood up. "Are you threatening me?"

Davis stood as well, bowing his chest out and pointing at Cal. "I'm warning you that you're venturing into dangerous territory—both professionally and personally. Consider what you are implying and who your lies might hurt."

"I consider that the truth might actually free some

people—and put the villain behind bars for good."

Davis' eyes narrowed. "We don't need people running around thinking such non-sense, Mr. Murphy. Let's preserve Carson Tanner's memory the way it should be—with honor, dignity, and respect."

"What I find disrespectful is your refusal to discuss that what happened was even possible by the right person with the technical know-how and the opportunity to make it happen."

Davis spit into his cup again. "People don't want to hear about that. They want to hear about what an amazing person Carson Tanner was—because he was. Attempting to convince everyone else that this was some elaborate murder plot is beyond ridiculous. That's the last thing I need right now."

"Exactly. It's the last thing you need right now, especially since you had plans to replace Tanner with Beaumont at the end of the season anyway. It keeps the suspicion off of you, even after you had already drawn up a contract to terminate Tanner."

Davis froze. "How'd you know about that?"

Cal laughed. "I didn't. But I do now."

Davis pointed toward the door. "You can see yourself out."

He waited until Cal left before burying his head in his hands. The stress was already taxing him. He picked up a pillow and slung it across the room.

That no-good reporter.

Were he not an owner, perhaps he would feel different and demand to know the truth. He picked up his phone and dialed a number. He had to make sure Cal's crazy theory remained unsubstantiated by NASCAR authorities—even if the meddling reporter was right.

CHAPTER 11

OWEN BURNS BOARDED the plane with his head down. He felt guilty that he wasn't mourning Carson Tanner more. Life would go on without his driver, but it was a stark reminder that tomorrow wasn't guaranteed. He would've preferred to cancel the remaining two races and take some time to reflect. But the rest of the world didn't live according to his druthers. It seemed to move faster than a race—and there was no time to stop.

He shuffled toward his row and settled into his assigned seat against the window. He glanced behind him to check on the rest of his crew.

"Where's Walters?" he asked.

"He upgraded to first class," Jackson Holmes said.

"What a punk."

If truth be told, Walters would rather sit in first class. He had the mileage to upgrade every time he set foot on a plane. But they were a team—and they needed to stick together, today more than ever.

The rest of the travelers piled onto the plane, while Burns tried to ignore the nagging in his mind. He wanted to get into the latest hot-selling novel sitting on his lap, but he couldn't. Not with Pat Walters acting pretentious. Today wasn't the time to bask in luxury—it was the time to be together. It was the time to share memories and lament. Maybe even laugh about good times with Tanner. But it wasn't the time to be isolated from everyone else.

Burns waited until it appeared the last passenger had boarded the flight. He waited another minute to calm down before he stormed toward the first class cabin.

A flight attendant blocked him a few rows shy of his intended destination. "Sir, I'm sorry, but you need to take a seat. We're about to take off."

He turned sideways and slipped past her. "This will only take a minute."

Burns located Walters and leaned over his seat. As he did so, he scanned the text message that Walters was busy hammering out on his phone.

"With Tanner finally out of the way…"

He'd read enough. Burns knelt down beside Walters. "What do you think you're doing?"

Walters turned and shuddered. With Burns just inches from his face, Walters was caught off guard. He turned off his phone and jammed it into his pocket.

"No need for discretion," Burns said. "I read what you wrote."

Walters glanced at his boss and rolled his eyes. "So what? Am I some kind of monster now?"

"You're definitely not a team player."

"And what makes you think that?"

Walters sighed. "You, sitting here. This is not the time to separate from everyone else. We need to stick together more than ever."

"What for? So we can cry about our driver who was

never going to win a championship?"

Burns shoved his finger in Walters' face. "Watch your mouth, son."

Walters slapped Burns' hand to the side and scoffed. "If you think Tanner was your meal ticket, you're dumber than you look. You know good and well he was never going to win a title."

"Maybe he would have if his throttle hadn't gotten stuck," Burns said and then paused. "And that was your responsibility to check, wasn't it?"

"Oh, fine. You wanna blame me now for a freak accident? You're a piece of work."

Burns refrained from taking a swing at Walters, but he didn't think twice about grabbing him by the scruff of his neck and getting in his face.

"Do you think this is some kind of joke?" Burns didn't wait for an answer. "Our driver died on the track and you're sending text messages about 'getting him out of the way.' This isn't a game, kid. This is real life with lives on the line. We don't play around when it comes to safety."

"If you want to accuse me, just come on out and say it, old timer," Walters snarled. "I don't have time for veiled accusations and innuendos."

Burns reared back and prepared to lunge toward Walters with a punch before a flight attendant tapped him on the shoulder.

"Sir, it's time to take your seat."

Burns nodded. "In a minute."

He knelt down next to Walters and got eye level with him, glaring at him the whole time. "You sorry, son of a gun. You disgust me."

With that, Burns rammed his fist into Walters' face.

Walters unbuckled his seat belt. He leapt to his feet and took a swing at Burns. It missed as his fist collided with another passenger's seatback.

"Gentlemen, please," the flight attendant barked.

Burns stopped to look at the woman, but Walters gave no such reprieve. Instead, the break in action was an opportunity for him to land a punch on an unguarded Burns.

Once Burns regained his bearings, he charged toward Walters, putting his head down into the middle of Walters' chest. He drove Walters all the way down the aisle and didn't stop until Walters' back rammed against the cockpit door.

One of the pilots flung the door to the cockpit open. "What's going on here? Enough!"

"I'm going to have to ask both of you to exit the plane," the flight attendant said.

Neither Walters nor Burns paid her any heed as their tussle led to the floor, where Burns landed on top of his subordinate. The two traded punches with Burns getting the better of Walters due to his position on top. Burns leaned back to avoid several punches from Walters before he landed a jarring right hand to the left side of Walters' face.

Burns stood to his feet and watched as Walters attempted to stand up. A few passengers gasped while other voiced their contempt for the altercation and belittled the two men. Obviously woozy from the hit, Walters staggered as he tried to get up before collapsing again. Burns then towered over his crew member.

"Is this how you wanna play this, son?" Burns said. "I can end your career right now with a couple of emails. Right now, this isn't about winning a championship—this is about respecting the dead. It's about respecting your friend. He may not have been the world's greatest driver, but he was a heckuva human being."

Walters looked up at him as he felt the blood oozing out of the corner of his mouth. "As bad of a driver as he was, Tanner was still a better human being than you'll ever be."

Burns pulled his hand back to unleash another punch before a pair of TSA security guards stormed on board and stopped him. They jerked Walters to his feet and led both men off the plane.

"Drivers don't just die in their race cars," Burns said. "That doesn't happen unless somebody is negligent."

Walters struggled to shake loose from the agent holding him. It was a fruitless attempt. "If you wanna blame me, just say it. I may not have seen eye-to-eye with Tanner, but I would never wish anyone dead. And I would've never acted negligently."

Burns sighed and shook his head. He stumbled forward at the urging of the guard behind him. "Maybe not, but you have a knack for overlooking things."

"Perhaps, but I'm not responsible for Tanner's death," Walters said.

"We'll see about that," Burns said, staggering forward at the behest of the guard behind him.

CHAPTER 12

CAL SLUMPED INTO THE CHAIR next to Eddie Simpson's desk and waited for him to end his phone conversation. Simpson held up his index finger to Cal and gave him a knowing nod. Cal tried not to look impatient as he glanced at his watch. He was only a few minutes early to his appointment with NASCAR's lead investigator on the Carson Tanner accident.

Never one to let an opportunity to glean information slip away, Cal tuned into Simpson's conversation. He pretended to ignore what was being said as he studied the cramped quarters of the NASCAR hauler and Simpson's makeshift office. It included a desk barely large enough to hold a framed family photo along with a University of Tennessee paperweight, which sat atop a mountain of haphazard files.

"Yes, I know it's a lot of money, but Emily would be heartbroken if I told her no," Simpson said to the person on the other line. "She might not be so heartbroken when she gets the bill for her student loans." He laughed. "Maybe I'm just delaying her outrage—but at least in four or five years from now she'll have a diploma from Duke to go along with her anger."

Simpson exchanged goodbyes and ended the call.

"So, Mr. Murphy, what can I do for you?" Simpson said as he folded his hands and leaned forward.

"I'm here to get some comments on the record about your investigation into the Carson Tanner accident," Cal said.

"There's not much to say, to be honest."

"Anything you care to go on record as saying?"

Simpson squinted and froze. "What exactly are you getting at?"

"Without going into too much detail, I've got sources telling me that there was nothing accidental about Tanner's crash on Sunday."

"So, what do you believe happened?"

"I think someone tampered with Tanner's car, causing him to hit the wall at a break-neck speed."

"He didn't break his neck."

"You know what I mean."

Simpson put his hands behind his head and leaned backward. "I'm not sure I do."

"What I'm trying to say is that the accident was no accident. It was an intentional act by someone to take Tanner out."

"Mr. Murphy, I know you haven't been covering our sport for very long, so let me explain something to you about how things work around race week. You just can't go gallivanting into the garage and start tinkering with engines. We have people guarding this area and we have regulations about when cars can be worked on. So, to suggest that someone could just walk in here and turn a team's car on its head with the twist of a wrench is absurd and highly unlikely at best."

Cal stared at Simpson and refused to blink. "Who said

anything about someone breaking into a garage?"

"Surely you aren't suggesting what I think you are."

Cal nodded. "Yes, I am. You obviously don't believe there's any way this was an inside job."

"And what makes you think that it was—if it wasn't an accident?"

"Just a hunch at this point, but it's a strong one."

Simpson laughed. "A hunch? Seriously? I hope you're not going to write that. Your readers will send you outta town on a rail, spewing garbage like that."

"I don't write anything until I have all the facts."

"That's reassuring because you're never going to be able to prove a ridiculous theory like that."

Cal scribbled a few notes on his pad. "Do you have any comment on the independent investigator that Mrs. Tanner hired to review your findings?"

"Our finding in this matter speaks for itself. I'm confident he won't find anything other than what we've already shared with the public."

Cal stood up and smiled. "Thank you for your time, Mr. Simpson. I'm sure we'll be talking again very soon."

***

CAL HEADED TO THE MEDIA CENTER and began banging away on his keyboard. Nobody was going to be happy with the story he was going to file. Not Ned Davis. Not NASCAR. Not his editor. But he reminded himself that he didn't write to please people—he wrote to inform them.

He slugged the headline: "Tanner Widow Questions Accident Report".

By Cal Murphy

PHOENIX — Jessica Tanner, the widow of driver Carson Tanner, has hired an independent investigator to review NASCAR officials' investigation into the cause of the fatal accident that killed the popular driver at the Texas Motors Speedway on Sunday.

NASCAR official Eddie Simpson welcomed the outside review but insisted that it won't reveal anything new.

"Our finding in this matter speaks for itself," Simpson said Thursday. "I'm confident (the investigator) won't find anything other than what we've already shared with the public."

Mrs. Tanner, who is unable to collect any life insurance since her husband's policy didn't cover track-related incidents unless it is proven that it wasn't an accident, insisted that the investigation had little to do with money.

"At the end of the day, I want to be able to put this horrible tragedy behind me with the full confidence of what actually happened," she said earlier this week. "This isn't about a life insurance settlement."

The private investigation is expected to release its findings before the end of the week.

Meanwhile, Davis Motor Sports has elected to finish out the race season with a new driver despite being unable to pick up any further points in the championship points race. Team owner Ned Davis has tagged up-and-coming driver J.T. Beaumont to pilot his team's car on Sunday in Phoenix.

Beaumont has won four races this season on lower circuits and has been rumored to be a candidate for several vacancies expected to open up at the end of the season.

Sources close to Davis indicated that Beaumont has long since been on the owner's short list, and that before last week's accident Davis had contemplated replacing Tanner with Beaumont after the season finale in Miami.

Cal hit send and looked at his watch. He set the over-under on getting a call back from Folsom at five minutes. Two minutes later, his cell phone buzzed.

Definitely should've taken the under.

"Good afternoon, Folsom," Cal said as he answered.

His editor wasn't in the mood for any pleasantries.

"What kind of grenades are you throwing with this piece, Cal? Are you insane? Do you want to burn every bridge we've ever built with Ned Davis?"

Cal took a deep breath and waited for Folsom to stop the onslaught of questions. "Are you done now?"

"I'm just gettin' started."

"Look, I know this seems a little brash, but something

is going on here and I need to entice someone to talk, maybe give them reason to step out of the shadows."

"And how exactly would this piece do that?"

"Do I really have to tell you that? You're fully aware that informants are less likely to be threatened when they speak out publicly."

Folsom grunted. "I think you're right there. Speaking out publicly makes them a target."

"If they feel like they're going to be a target, I can always protect them."

"I'd be more worried about you than an informant at that point."

"I understand what you're saying, but I wouldn't stick my neck out like this if I didn't think there was more to this story."

"Think about it, Cal. If what you're suggesting is true and someone was able to sabotage Tanner's car and make it appear like an accident, what makes you think they couldn't do the same to you?"

"Then it'd be real suspicious, wouldn't it?"

"And maybe you'd be dead."

"Oh, come on—"

"This is no joke, Cal. If you want me to run this, I will. I'll take some of the heat for you, but you best be prepared for the blowback on this. It won't be pretty."

Cal sighed. "It wouldn't be the first time I've stirred up trouble for myself with my reporting."

"You're not invincible—just remember that."

CHAPTER 13

RON PARKER ASSUMED HIS POST just outside the garage gate in the infield of the Phoenix International Raceway. Armed with nothing more than a radio to communicate with security officials, he slid onto his stool and opened up the latest David Baldacci novel and began reading.

There could be worse things to do on a Friday morning.

He wished he could disappear like the main character in the book and go off the grid. At least he could sleep in peace, devoid of any nightmares about being found and tortured—or perhaps even killed. But he couldn't leave Nancy, not like that. She'd been too good to him, as evidenced by the fact that she was with him on this ruse of a retirement hobby. The first year was fine, but the traveling circus began to wear on him midway through this season year—as did the threats.

He glanced down at his cell phone, the black case glistening beneath the beading desert sun. As he ran his fingers across the buttons, he contemplated how long he would have the phone before he'd have to discard it. He didn't bother programming any numbers into it. He'd entered the numbers of his friends into so many burner phones that he now knew them all by heart.

A reporter walked past him and flashed his pit pass. Parker waived him through.

Parker tried reading to pass the time but couldn't focus after coming across a passage about a man who thought he was safe only to be dragged away moments later by a team of thugs.

Is this to be my fate?

He closed the book and tried to think about something else, *anything* else. The scoreboard in the middle of the track flickered with drivers' times. He tried to predict which of those drivers near the top would win the upcoming race. If he'd learned anything about racing, it was that the fastest car didn't *always* win; but if you weren't in the top fifteen during qualifying, you wouldn't be challenging anyone for the victory on race day.

Several crew members approached the gate and displayed their passes. He stood up and allowed them to enter.

He glanced up at the cloudless sky before he felt his phone buzz in his pocket.

Must be Nancy. She's the only one who has this number.

Parker made a habit of reprogramming her phone when she wasn't looking. She never bothered to look at the number once she discovered the ease of pushing a button, speaking his name, and waiting a moment before it called him.

He dug his phone out and stared at the number. It wasn't Nancy or any number he recognized.

What the—

"Hello?" he answered.

"Nice of you to pick up, Parker," the voice said.

"Now, listen, I told you I'm going to get you your money, but you have to give me some time."

"Oh, you're all out of time. Now that I know where you are, I'm comin' for you. And, Parker?"

"Yes?"

"The price just went up."

The line went dead.

Parker wiped his forehead with the back of his hand and slumped on top of his stool.

Deep breath, deep breath.

He looked at his hand, which wouldn't stop shaking.

What am I gonna do?

Parker scanned the asphalt in front of him. There wasn't a soul in sight. He turned around and looked over his shoulder into the garage area. He saw a familiar face. At least, he thought he did.

Is that him?

He squinted as he turned all the way around and peered into the garage area.

I swear that's the guy.

Parker pulled out his phone and tried to snap a picture. Before he could get a close enough view, the man vanished around a stack of tires.

He wanted to find that reporter again, let him know who was tinkering on Tanner's car on Sunday morning. But not now.

Parker had a different idea, a better one—one that could make all his problems go away.

CHAPTER 14

CAL SHUFFLED TOWARD HIS SEAT on press row in the media center. He tossed his computer bag on the table and headed toward the media buffet. As he squeezed past another writer reading the comments section of an article he had written, Cal stopped and leaned over his shoulder.

"You'll live a lot longer if you don't read those," Cal said.

The writer nodded and smiled. "I read them purely for entertainment."

"You need a new hobby."

Cal headed outside and took a spot at the back of the line.

"Just the person I wanted to see," he said.

Sylvia Yates, the Davis Motor Sports media relations manager, turned around. "Cal Murphy—as I live and breathe. I can't believe you're still alive."

He shook his head. "I take it you read my article from yesterday."

"Read it? I had to deal with the fallout of it. Thanks to you, my easy Thursday was ruined. Everybody wanted to talk to Ned about what you wrote."

"I hope it didn't upset him."

"Oh, no," she said, shaking her head. "Upset is far too mild of a word. And the more accurate word is not one appropriate for a lady to utter in public."

"Every word of it was true."

She wagged her finger at him. "Those sneaky little un-named sources."

"They can be little flies in the ointment, can't they?"

"Apparently, not for you. They're more like the spice of life—or the crux of your story."

Cal picked up a paper plate and a plastic fork wrapped in a napkin. "Sylvia, you ought to know by now that I don't make things up."

She nodded. "Maybe, but I'm very suspicious of re-porters when they start quoting unnamed sources."

"Does this mean my interview with J.T. Beaumont is off?"

She eyed him cautiously before selecting a deli sandwich off a large platter. "No, I wouldn't do that to you. But you must realize you've put me in a precarious situation with your story."

"Is Ned cracking the whip?"

"Let's just say it's best that you avoid him for a while."

"I'm not trying to bust anybody's chops, okay? My job is to report what's happening out there."

Sylvia grabbed a cookie off the dessert tray. "I under-stand that, but I have a boss who pays me to control the nar-rative. And it's getting away from him right now."

"Maybe he shouldn't have been so loose with his lips." Cal gestured toward a table and allowed Sylvia to lead the way.

"What are you trying to say?"

"I'm saying I've got audio of Ned Davis talking about J.T. Beaumont and Carson Tanner. His comments about

Tanner are—how should I say this—less than sympathetic."

They both sat down at the table. Cal dug into his sandwich and glanced at the cars speeding around the track on practice runs.

"I think you need to stop," she said.

"Stop what?"

"Stop writing about this story."

Cal leaned back, his brow furrowed. "And why would I do that? I'm just publishing facts."

"Yeah, well, Ned Davis can make your life difficult."

Cal eyed her cautiously. "That almost sounds like a threat."

"I'm simply warning you about what might happen if you continue on this path. Look, there might be something suspicious going on—or maybe not. I understand you have to get your answers. But don't come looking to me for them. I like Mr. Davis and I like my job. Understand?"

Cal nodded.

She continued. "I once thought I had an opportunity to work for another team."

Cal wiped his mouth with his napkin. "Which one?"

"I'm not going to tell you, but it was one of the best teams out there."

"So what happened?"

"I didn't get the job."

"There's no shame in that. You're in a competitive field."

She shook her head. "No, it's not like that. Some rumors began to circulate about me—the kind of rumors that no one wants to hear."

"Untrue, I'm assuming?"

"Completely fabricated."

"So, who made them up?"

She picked at her salad with her fork. "I can't be sure, but the only thing I know is that there was only one person who benefitted from the spreading of such rumors."

"Ned Davis?"

"The one and only."

"Sorry to hear that."

She took a drink of water from the bottle in front of her. "Yeah, well, this job still pays well for the time being. I'd like to dip my toes in the water and see what else is out there, but I'm stuck for now. Ned thinks very highly of me and when his offers to pay me more don't pan out, he resorts to other tactics to keep me tethered to him." She paused. "Don't get me wrong—I like what I do. But at this point, I'm more fearful of what might happen if I try to leave to work for someone else. I love racing and want to be involved in this sport."

"So, you're saying he's got a thing for you?"

She smiled. "That's one way of putting it."

"That's too bad," Cal said. He put his head down and focused on his meal.

"What's too bad?" said another woman.

Cal looked up and locked eyes with Alexa Jennings, Davis' girlfriend.

"Huh?"

"What's too bad?" Alexa asked again.

"Oh, nothing."

"Well, if I were you, Cal, I'd listen to Sylvia. She knows how to handle Ned—maybe even more so than I do.

"Do you know what we were even talking about?" Cal asked.

"I can only imagine," Alexa said before flitting toward the buffet table.

He turned toward Sylvia and leaned in close. "And then you have to deal with her?"

"She's the one you ought to be talking to. If anyone knows what's going on, she does."

Cal nodded. "Text me the next time she's alone in the hauler. I have a few questions for her."

CHAPTER 15

RON PARKER WAITED until his lunch break to trudge toward the Davis Motor Sports hauler. He'd visited with several members of the crew before, enough to be recognized as someone other than a groupie.

"Can I help you?" Owen Burns asked as Parker approached the truck.

"I was hoping to speak to Mr. Davis," he answered.

"Do you have an appointment?"

Parker shook his head. "I don't, but tell him it's important."

"Stay right there."

Several moments later, Burns re-emerged from the hauler with Ned Davis trailing behind him. Burns moved to the side as Davis stepped forward.

"I'm sorry. Have we met?" Davis asked, extending his hand toward Parker.

Parker grabbed his hand and shook it. "We spoke several weeks ago. I work for your trailer that sells all the Davis Motor Sports merchandise."

Davis nodded. "Oh, yes, I remember now. What can I do for you, Mister—"

"Parker. Ron Parker."

"Yes, Mr. Parker. How can I help you?"

"I had something I wanted to talk with you about, but it's kind of private in nature. Can we go somewhere else?"

Davis motioned for him to follow. "I've got just the place."

Parker followed him inside the hauler and into the cramped office. Davis waited for his guest to enter the room before pulling the door shut behind him. He motioned to Parker to have a seat.

"So, Mr. Parker, what can I do for you?"

Parker shifted in his seat. "Well, there's something you need to know about—something very important."

"And what's that?"

"I know who sabotaged Carson Tanner's car last week."

Jolted by the accusation, Davis sat back. "Sabotaged?"

"That crash on Sunday was no accident."

Davis rolled his eyes and threw his hands in the air. "Is there an idiot virus outbreak that I'm not aware of? Geez, I swear if another person tries to sell me that pack of lies today, I'm gonna—"

"With all due respect, sir, I'm not making this up."

"And why should I believe you? Do you have proof?"

"I know what I saw."

Davis slapped his knee and glared at Parker. "Do you have a picture of what you saw?"

"Not with me."

Davis shook his head. "So what do you want? Money? A job?"

"Fifty grand in cash."

"Are you out of your mind?"

Parker held his ground. "I'm doing you a favor, sir—and

giving you a deal to boot. I could fetch twice that from some news outlet hungry to get exclusive rights."

"So, why come to me, oh great Patron Saint of NASCAR Sabotage?"

"I like you and I think you'll do the right thing with the information that I give you."

Davis leaned back and sighed. "And what do you think is the right thing to do?"

"Blackball this soon-to-be former employee of yours and quietly remove him before he costs another driver his life—all while avoiding the public relations nightmare that would ensue if I went elsewhere with this information."

"Okay, I might agree to your little extortion plan, but I need time to get the money. However, I'm not giving you a dime until I see physical evidence. No picture, no money. Got it?"

Parker nodded.

"Meet me back here at eight o'clock tomorrow morning and we'll make the exchange."

Parker exited the hauler and exhaled.

Maybe I should've asked for more.

He knew that would've been greedy, and getting those thugs off his back once and for all would be payment enough. Now all he had to do was find that phone he'd thrown out the window.

CHAPTER 16

TODD CASHMAN CLIMBED into his car and tightened his grip on the steering wheel. Thanks to his win in Texas, his place in the championship race was secure. There were a handful of drivers with a shot to qualify for the remaining three slots open for the final race in Miami, several of whom Cashman despised. This week's race was more about bumping some tougher competitors out—and proving a point.

He revved up his engine and prepared for his pole laps. All he needed was a few good runs and he'd take pole position. It wasn't like he needed it, but he needed everyone to know that he was there to win, no matter how secure his place was. Winning trumped everything each and every week. If any of the other drivers thought he might be taking it easy, they'd be mistaken.

His car roared onto the track and hit 143.014 miles per hour on his second lap around the track.

"New track record," said one of his spotters over the radio.

"I like it," Cashman said. "But I ain't done yet."

Cashman jammed his foot onto the accelerator again and readied for another run.

"Is this really necessary?" his crew chief asked. "Nobody's gonna top that."

"Just getting a feel for the track and this new set up," Cashman answered. "Good thing you guys got me on your team."

Cashman guided his car around the track three more times before deciding to call it quits, never nearing his record-breaking lap time again.

He switched over to his private channel as he pulled onto pit row.

"You want to make some adjustments?" his crew chief asked.

"I think we're good." He paused. "Is Beaumont driving the No. 39 car this week?"

"Yep."

"I still owe that little punk. Remember what he did to me two years ago?"

"How could I forget? You remind me constantly."

"Time to welcome him to the show."

His crew chief protested. "Can't that wait until Sunday?"

Cashman decided to get in close to Beaumont's car, which was also pitted. As he veered closer to Beaumont, one of the Davis Motor Sports crew members nearly stepped in his path. Cashman laughed as he blew past them—and all the while unaware that he nearly hit someone.

Cashman slithered out of his car to find Beaumont's entire crew standing just a few feet behind his pit. The Davis crew immediately started jawing with Cashman and his team, trading insults and obscene gestures. Before Cashman could get over the wall and find out what was happening, one of his crew members landed a sucker punch on one of Beaumont's guys. Within seconds, fists and elbows started flying. The crew members brawled for about a minute before

NASCAR officials and several other teams' crew members helped pull the men off each other.

Cashman shook his head as Beaumont's crew meandered back toward their pit.

"What was that all about?" he asked.

"You," his crew chief answered.

"Me? What'd I do?"

"You almost ran over one of their guys." He glared at Cashman. "Keep your cool next time. Got it?"

***

OWEN BURNS RUBBED his face and took a deep breath. Managing the fragile egos of all the crew members on his team proved taxing work, far more difficult than rescheduling a pair of flights the day before. While he had cooled down from the previous day's confrontation and he and Ross had come to an amicable agreement to stay out of each other's way, now he had to deal with a bunch of hot heads who were ready to trade punches after Todd Cashman's antics on pit road. He ushered everyone back to the team hauler to deal with the fallout. They all filed into the cramped room.

"Settle down," Burns said. "No need in anyone getting suspended over that hot head's move. Let's take out our anger by getting our race car in tip-top shape, not in taking shots at Cashman's crew."

Russ Ross stood up. "Well, not everyone was taking shots."

Burns furrowed his brow and stared at Ross.

Ross continued. "Some people just stood back and let

everyone else do the dirty work." He fixated his gaze on Pat Walters. "Dirt decided not to join his teammates."

"Now, wait a minute, Ross," Burns interjected. "The last thing we need is for you to start slinging around accusations."

"Too late that for that, boss. Didn't you read that article this morning? Apparently someone on this team isn't exactly a team player and sabotaged our car last week."

Burns sighed and shook his head. "Yeah, I read it. It's horse crap, and you know it, Ross. Just chill out, okay?"

Ross sat down. "I doubt I was the only one who noticed."

"I noticed," Jackson Holmes chimed in. "Nice to know who's got your back—and who doesn't."

"You guys are crazy—" Dirt said.

"All right, all right. Settle down, everyone. It's not worth getting upset about it at this point."

Ross stood up again. "Oh, yeah? Well, I take issue with anyone who tinkers with one of *my* cars."

Then Dirt stood up. "What are you tryin' to say?"

"If the message isn't coming across loud and clear by now, you're deaf as a doorpost."

Dirt didn't bother responding. Instead, he reared back and took a swing at Ross, who landed an uppercut that spawned a bloody lip for Dirt.

Burns stepped in and pushed them back to opposite sides of the room. "Enough, you two. This is no way to treat your teammate."

Ross felt his jaw. "It's no way to treat your driver either, no matter how many races he chokes away."

Burns stamped his foot. "Shut up—both of you. We all

know that report was a lie. Tanner died in a tragic accident, but no one here had anything to do with it. We can blame each other and point fingers, or we can grab each other around the neck and hug. We're a team—let's act like it."

After delivering a pep talk for several more minutes, Burns stepped out of the hauler to check his phone. It had been buzzing for the past several minutes.

He noticed an abnormally high amount of voice mail messages. He growled as he listened to the first two—both of them identical in nature. They both sought his opinion on the fight that happened on pit road and wanted to know if he noticed if Dirt chose not to get involved in the fracas.

Then he opened his Twitter app. It was lit up with links and comments about a blog pointing out how Dirt had sat out the fight.

"Is This the Saboteur?" one blog post link asked.

Given the circumstances, Burns thought it was a fair question—but one he already knew the answer to.

CHAPTER 17

CAL GLANCED AT THE final results from that afternoon's pole as he strolled along pit road. After the fracas, he couldn't help but smile at the two drivers occupying the top slots: Todd Cashman and J.T. Beaumont. *Can the drama get any better than this?* He knew it couldn't, and it added another scintillating storyline to Sunday's upcoming race.

Not that he needed more storylines to cover. NASCAR got what it hoped for when it changed the way it determined its champion. Culling pretenders from contenders each week during the final ten races led to more competitive driving and created tension the sport had never before experienced. The previous format of adding up points based on where a driver finished over the long grind of a season fell short in creating the kind of winner-take-all atmosphere that resonated with American sports fans.

And Cal enjoyed the changes—except when it meant more work.

His phone buzzed. It was Folsom.

"I wasn't expecting to hear from you so soon," Cal said as he answered.

"We've got some early deadlines tonight and I need your stories within the hour."

"What? No lecture about how my article created a firestorm of work for you and an impromptu chewing out from your boss?"

Folsom chuckled. "It's still early."

"Well, let the record show that I was right. I'm sure you have plenty of web traffic statistics to soften the blow."

"That story set a record for our NASCAR coverage," Folsom mumbled.

"What was that? I didn't quite hear you."

"All right, enough gloating. You know I was more concerned with how it would affect your relationships with the people you're covering."

Cal shook his head. "That's what you said, anyway."

"Well, did it?"

"So far, so good," Cal said. "But I've got to get a few comments from some drivers for my pole story, so I guess I'll find out shortly."

"And comments about the clash on pit road as well, I hope. I'm counting on a sidebar from you on that."

"Has anyone ever called you a slave driver?"

"Every single day. Now get to work."

"Later." Cal hung up and climbed the steps leading to the second floor of the media center. He scratched down a few notes and questions on his pad before heading downstairs and toward the garage.

As he attempted to enter the garage area, a security official stopped him.

"Excuse me, sir, but you're not allowed into the garage area at this time," the official said.

Cal furrowed his brow and watched as another journalist slipped past him into the garage. He gestured toward the person who walked past him. "But *he* gets to go in?"

"Sorry, man. I'm just doing my job. You need a hot pit pass to get into the garage right now."

"The garage isn't hot," Cal protested. When cars were still on the track, the garage area was considered "hot" and access was restricted. Cal understood the distinction but didn't hear any cars roaring around the track.

The man pointed toward the yellow flashing light affixed to the top of the fence above his head. "If that's blinking, it's hot. Just doin' my job."

Cal held up his press credential and shook it. "I haven't had a problem with this all week."

"Look, mister, if you don't like it, go get the appropriate pass," the man said as he fished a folded sheet of paper out of his pocket. He unfolded it and pointed to a row of passes that granted access to the garage area when it was hot. "This is yours," he said, pointing to a row of passes that were not allowed to access the garage area when it was considered hot.

As the security official began to fold up the paper, another sheet of paper fell out of his pocket. Before he could bend down to pick it up, another voice squawked on his walkie-talkie with a question for him.

Cal knelt down and picked up the piece of paper. But when he did, he noticed something.

This handwriting looks familiar.

With his phone in his hand, Cal snapped a quick photo before returning it to the security official.

The man nodded and mouthed a "thank you" to Cal as he continued to listen to the official on the other end.

Once the man finished his conversation, Cal put his arm

on his shoulder. "I'll be back with the proper pass."

Cal headed for the media center to request a hot pit pass. While he was waiting to get clearance, he pulled out the note someone slipped into his pocket after the race and compared the handwriting to the picture he'd taken of the piece of paper that fell onto the ground.

A perfect match.

Pulled back to the present when a media relations assistant handed him a pass, Cal thanked the man and returned to the gate.

Cal held up his new pass for the security official to see.

The man pointed to the yellow light above the gate that was no longer on. "It doesn't matter now." He smiled and waived Cal through.

But Cal stopped. He whispered in the man's ear. "I know who you are. You mind telling me why you slipped that note into my pocket last week in Texas?"

The man froze as Cal stepped back. "What are you talking about?"

"Don't play dumb with me. I know it was you." Cal grabbed the man's identification badge. "Mr. Parker. Mr. Ron Parker."

Parker snatched the badge out of Cal's hand and covered it with his hand. "I don't know what you're talking about."

"Oh, I think you do. It's written all over your face. You thought Carson Tanner's crash wasn't an accident. And you left me a note that told me so." Cal held up the note between his fingers. "But you wanted to do so anonymously. It's too late for that now. So, tell me, Mr. Parker, what did you see?"

Parker glanced around as if he was looking for someone. "Look, I can't talk right now." He paused and looked down at his feet. "But you're right—I did see something. I even have proof."

Cal leaned in close and spoke through his teeth in a hushed voice. "Do you have any idea what you're suggesting?"

Parker leaned back and nodded. "You obviously do too since you wrote about it."

"That's a thread to this story I can't tug on without more proof. Do you want to let some killer just roam free—if that's really what happened?"

Parker waived through several journalists. "I've got proof and I can get it to you. But not right now. Meet me tonight at my RV and I'll show it to you." He proceeded to give Cal directions.

"What time?" Cal asked.

"Late. Let's say ten o'clock. I've got some business I need to take care of first."

Cal nodded. "Fair enough. And don't worry, Mr. Parker. I'll protect you—and I can protect you more so than if you go to the cops."

Parker scanned the area behind Cal. "The cops are the least of my concern at this point."

Cal's eyes narrowed as he tilted his head. "Are you in some kind of danger?"

"Just a little nervous—that's all."

CHAPTER 18

JESSICA TANNER STARED at the piece of paper in front of her in disbelief. A couple of tears trickled off her cheeks and splashed onto the document. It was the result she wanted to see—but she didn't want to see it either.

She looked up from the paper and wiped her eyes. "Artificially stressed? Does that mean what I think it means?"

The investigator nodded. "If you look close enough, you can determine if someone stressed a part or if it was just due to the rigorous wear and tear of a long race. The return spring that's supposed to make the throttle come back was exposed to far more heat than it should have been."

She sniffled. "Even after the fire?"

"The fire was out before it got started. And that kind of heat looks different. I think someone stressed this with heat before the race."

She nodded and started crying again.

"I'm really sorry, m'am."

Jessica nodded. "Thank you. I think I need to be alone now."

She ushered the investigator out and locked the door behind him. Then she collapsed onto the floor in a blubbering mess.

After regaining her composure, she picked up her cell phone and called Cal Murphy.

"Hi, Jessica. How are you?" he said as he answered.

"I don't know," she said, trying to keep from falling apart again. "I just got the report back from the investigator."

"And?"

"He found evidence that the return spring was artificially stressed." She broke down and started bawling.

He waited until she regained her composure. "Can you email me a copy of it so I can look at it and take it to the NASCAR officials here?"

She took a deep breath. "Sure."

"Thanks. I'll see what I can do with this information and keep you posted." He paused. "You're a brave woman, Jessica. I know this isn't easy for you, but if this is true, we need to catch this person and stop him from doing it again."

***

CAL IMMEDIATELY DIALED Folsom's number to tell him the breaking news.

Folsom picked up and Cal barely waited for him to utter a word.

"Tanner's widow just called me with the findings of the independent investigator." He didn't wait for Folsom to comment. "The return spring was tampered with."

"I'm assuming you think that's what caused the wreck then?"

"No doubt about it. We've got a murder on our hands."

"Send me what you've got as soon as you can."

Cal sighed. "As much as I want to, I want to wait."

"For what?"

"I want to take this to NASCAR and see what they say about it."

Folsom moaned. "Come on, Cal. Let's get this out there now. We don't want to get scooped on this story. You know it's gonna be a firestorm when it hits."

"Exactly. So, let's give NASCAR a chance to respond. Besides, who else is going to find out about this unless you're the one spreadin' the news?"

"You trust Jessica Tanner that much? You think you're the only journalist she's talking to?"

"I'm not sure, but I wanna get a story, not a headline."

"Fine, but I'm giving you a deadline of eight o'clock your time to get me something so I can fit it on the front page. Otherwise, I'm running the headline and calling Jessica Tanner myself."

"You'll have a story—don't worry."

Cal hung up and looked at his phone, which had buzzed during his call with Folsom. A number he didn't recognize appeared on his caller ID—and there was a message.

"Hi, Mr. Murphy. This is Alexa Jennings, Ned Davis' girl-friend. I know you've spoken with Ned about the possibility that someone tampered with Carson's car before the race last week. Please don't tell him I told you this because he'd kill me, but I just can't stand to see him stick his head in the sand about this. I need you to meet me because I have some information about who might have done this. Call me back."

Cal scrolled through his phone to find her number and dialed her number.

"Hi, Ms. Jennings, this is Cal Murphy. You left me a message earlier. Is this a good time for you to talk?"

"Hang on a second, let me step outside," she said.

Cal waited for several moments as he heard the scuffling of feet and then the clink of a hauler door latching shut.

"Okay, now I can talk."

"So, what's this all about."

"It's about Owen Burns," she said. "I think he's the one who did it—and I've got proof."

CHAPTER 19

OWEN BURNS CRACKED OPEN a beer and slumped into his chair inside the Davis Motor Sports hauler. He was ready for the season to be over. With nothing to race for but pride, he wished his boss would've just ended the season two weeks early and let everyone grieve and rest.

"We've got contracts to fulfill," Davis had told him a few days earlier.

"It's always about the money, isn't it?" Burns smacked his hand against the wall and walked out.

He didn't need to wait around for Davis to tell him the answer he already knew. NASCAR was the king at making money, innovators in professional sports. While the rest of pro sports relied on ticket sales to make money in the early days, NASCAR had figured out a way to monetize everything, all for the good of the sport. Tracks sprang up and became iconic monuments around the country. Racecars were designed to run faster. Drivers became more intelligent. Crews grew more equipped.

"Things have changed, Burns," Davis yelled after him. "This ain't your granddaddy's racing."

Burns drained the beer and went for another. As he did, Alexa Jennings stomped on top of the cooler, stopping him short of his intended goal.

"Sure you wanna drink another one?" she asked.

He eyed her cautiously. "My liver wouldn't mind a break."

She slipped her foot off. "Good. You get into all kinds of trouble when you start drinkin' around here."

He rolled his eyes and sat back down. She reached for the door and looked back at him once more before exiting the room.

Burns got up and grabbed another beer. "What's her problem?" he asked aloud.

Ross walked into the room. "Were you sayin' something?"

Burns shook his head. "Nah, just tryin' to deal with that overbearing girlfriend of Ned's."

"I know how I'd like to deal with her," Ross said.

Burns waved him off. "You're sick, you know that? I bet if she got close enough to a fire, her face would melt. She ain't real—and she's old enough to be your mother."

"Fine by me. I'm a cub."

"You're an idiot—that's what you are, especially if you attempt to put the moves on your boss's girlfriend."

"To each his own," Burns said before finishing the rest of his beer.

They sat in silence for a moment before Burns spoke again.

"Sorry about all that drama on the plane."

"Aww, forget about it, man. I don't care what you do now as long as you keep me on this team."

"Why's that?"

Ross scratched his chest and took the last swig of his

drink. "Because we finally got a driver who can win us a championship."

Burns shot him a look. "Don't go celebratin' just yet. We ain't won a title, much less a race. We don't know how the kid's gonna do on Sunday or how he'll handle an entire season of racing next year."

"I doubt he'll choke like Tanner, God rest his soul."

"Hey!" Burns threw a crumpled can at Ross. "Don't speak ill of the dead. You know that's bad luck."

Ross laughed and stood up before tossing the can back to Burns. "We make our own luck in this world."

"Tanner never hurt anybody," Burns quipped. "He was a good man and he didn't deserve to die."

"True—but it might be the best thing that ever happened to this team."

***

SYLVIA YATES CROUCHED against a door inside the hauler and glanced around. With no one in sight, she strained to hear the conversation taking place in the room next door. She looked around again and decided to better position herself to hear more clearly. Before she could rethink her decision, she pressed her ear against the door and could hear the entire conversation between Russ Ross and Owen Burns. After a few minutes, she'd heard enough. She then took a deep breath and dialed the number for Alayna French.

After working together for several years in the NASCAR corporate office, Sylvia and Alayna both landed jobs with race teams. Alayna intended to stay on longer with NASCAR, but she couldn't resist the opportunity to brag about her prominent promotion on Twitter. The next morning, she was asked to pack up her belongings six weeks before she planned on it.

Sylvia, however, kept her mouth shut. She recognized the volatility of the industry as soon as she entered it and vowed to avoid scorching bridges during her transition from one job to the next. But Alayna still hadn't learned that lesson, a fact Sylvia remembered when she needed to leak some important information.

However, this wasn't information she wanted to leak; rather, it was a message. She wanted to let Cal Murphy know that his hunch was right. It wouldn't take much to entice Alayna to pass the cryptic message along.

"What's up, Syl?" Alayna answered.

Sylvia bit her tongue. She hated it when Alayna called her by that lame nickname. "Have you seen Cal Murphy from *The Observer* around?"

"Yeah, I spoke with him this afternoon. What's up?"

"Oh, I haven't seen him today, but I'm looking for him. I wanted to let him know that he's got the green light on that story we were talking about earlier, but I can't reach him."

"And you've tried his cell?"

"Yeah, but I can't get an answer."

"Hmmm," Alayna said. "That's weird. I saw him texting on his phone today at lunch."

"Well, if you see him, tell him to give me a call, will ya?"

"Sure thing."

Sylvia hung up and turned her phone off. She never intended to answer a call from Cal Murphy. No need to leave a trail back to her once Ned Davis flushed out who might have told him the truth about what his team was really up to.

CHAPTER 20

RON PARKER CHECKED his mirrors and set his cruise control for the highest acceptable speed without getting caught. If he was honest with himself, he was less worried about getting stopped by the Arizona State Highway Patrol than he was someone else.

Just breathe, Ron.

He took a deep breath and shifted in his seat. With a long ride ahead of him, he decided to turn on the radio and get lost in a song or two.

Bruce Springsteen's "Born to Run" blared on the first station he tuned into. He hit scan to search for another channel. Pink's "So What" came on the next one.

He found himself singing along to the catchy tune. *I'm gonna start a fight.* And then he stopped.

Parker wanted to end the possibility that he might get into a fight, the kind of fight where only one person won. And he doubted it would be him.

He turned the radio off and checked his rearview mirror again. A light flickered in the distance as he switched lanes.

Am I being followed?

Parker resigned himself to the fact that he was nothing more than paranoid, not that he blamed himself. Gambling was a bad habit with dire consequences—if you didn't keep winning. He couldn't remember the last time he won, which led to his sad state of affairs. In a matter of months, he rolled up $40,000 in losses just prior to his retirement. Foolishly, he believed he could double or triple the money, padding the modest nest egg he'd managed to accumulate for Nancy and himself. Reality was coming back to extricate payment—and pain.

He glanced again in the mirror. The car behind him seemed to speed up as the traffic exiting the city thinned with each exit. Before too long, he passed the last bedroom community to Phoenix and was headed deep into the desert in search of his cell phone.

At least it will all be over after this.

He checked his watch. He doubted he'd make it back in time to meet the reporter. That was his backup plan. Cal Murphy wouldn't have time to write a story until after he'd received his money from Ned Davis. And even if Davis suspected him, it's not like he'd make that public or complain about it. Parker surmised that even more suspicion would be cast Davis's way if he tried to do something to him.

Ninety minutes into his errand, Parker decided he needed some coffee. He eyed his mirror again. There were a few cars way behind him. He exhaled and relaxed. When the next exit rolled up on him three miles later he pulled off, glancing once more into his mirror to see if any cars followed him. They didn't.

This ought to be simple enough.

He pulled into a truck stop and trudged inside. The coffee choices turned Parker's stomach, but this wasn't about luxury—it was about survival. He needed a warm cup to keep him company for the remaining drive ahead that night.

To pass the time, he recalled aloud the drivers who had won the championships in chronological order.

1978, Cal Yarborough. 1979, Richard Petty. 1980, Dale Earnhardt. 1981, Darrell Waltrip. 1982, Darrell Waltrip. 1983, Bobby Allison.

He stopped. Exit 303.

Parker put his flashers on and got out of his car. Armed with a flashlight, he began combing the desert brush along the I-10 for his phone. Calling the old phone would do no good since the battery was surely dead.

For ten minutes, he walked over the area in search of the phone until he finally spotted it.

Bingo!

As he reached down to pick it up, Parker heard a sound he dreaded. A rapid clicking sound. He froze and slowly turned to look behind him with the phone securely in his hand. He shined the light on the ground behind him and confirmed his suspicions. A rattlesnake.

Parker slid the phone into his pocket and contemplated his next move. He knew rattlesnakes weren't the world's fastest animals, but there weren't many things slower than him. He decided to back up slowly and keep the light trained on the snake. After several steps backward, the snake didn't move. *Just a few more steps.* It didn't move. Confident that he had the head start he needed to reach his car about twenty yards away, Parker decided to turn and run.

He didn't make it back to his car before he felt a searing pain shoot up his leg.

Parker shook his leg and flung the snake into the road. He hurried into his car and checked his leg. It hurt but it didn't look like the bite was too deep or long.

He turned the ignition on his car as it roared to life. Without another thought, he drove across the median and headed back toward Phoenix. He knew he needed to have it looked at by a doctor in an emergency room just thirty minutes west of his location in Tucson.

Nancy would never understand … or forgive me.

He'd just grit it out. He stomped on the accelerator and clenched his teeth.

CHAPTER 21

CAL GROWLED WHEN HIS CALL to Sylvia Yates went straight to voicemail. She always had her phone on, so something seemed off other than just her phone. *If she wanted to talk to me, she wouldn't be avoiding me, so what gives?* He climbed the steps of the media center and sat down at one of the outside tables.

He reviewed what Alayna French told him. Alayna had said, *"Sylvia told me to tell you that you had the green light to continue working on that story and to call her."*

Not that he needed her permission, but her blessing on a story of this nature made for a more desirable working relationship.

Cal mulled over what to do for a few minutes before deciding to make a visit to the Davis Motor Sports hauler. Perhaps he could talk to her in person or—even better—talk to Alexa Jennings.

When Cal inquired as to Sylvia's whereabouts, no one knew. The driver for the hauler said he'd seen her a few minutes ago, but she left for some sponsorship appearance.

Cal put his hands on his hips and surveyed the garage. Crews scurried around making final adjustments or cleaning up for the day. Nothing seemed out of the ordinary. Some of the haulers looked desolate, apparently finished for the afternoon. He continued scanning the garage when he felt a tap on his shoulder.

He spun around to find Alexa Jennings behind him.

"Lookin' for a scoop, Mr. Newspaper Man?" she said.

Cal stepped back and stared at Alexa. He figured she must've been a raving beauty at one point in her life and manipulated men to get what she wanted through a variety of conniving methods. Now, she relied on thick makeup, Botox, hair extensions and several obvious enhancements to continue getting her way. Cal wouldn't be beguiled.

"I'd settle for the opportunity to show my editor that I wasn't crazy with the accusations I levied about what happened to Carson Tanner," he said.

She smiled and stepped forward, infringing on his personal space. She straightened the collar on his Oxford shirt and patted his chest several times. "I bet you would."

Cal took another step back. "Look, Ms. Jennings, I'm not interested in whatever it is you're doing, but I am interested in what you told me earlier."

She wagged her finger at him and clucked her tongue. "All work and no play makes for a dull Cal Murphy." She encroached on him again.

Cal stepped back twice and laughed. "No one ever accused me of being a barrel of fun." He paused. "Except my wife, to whom I'm happily married."

She rolled her eyes. "Fine. Be that way." She turned around and started walking in the opposite direction.

"If you don't want to give me that proof you told me about, that's fine by me. I only come by my information honestly."

She cackled. "Is that so? People just bare their souls to you and you make them anonymous sources."

He nodded. "That's kinda how it works—and I'm not ashamed of it. I've prided myself on handling sources that way for years in touchy situations. I can offer you that same sort of protection, if that's what you need."

"There's only one person who's going to need protection once this story breaks." She stopped and continued in a whisper, "Owen Burns."

Cal sighed. "So, tell me about this proof."

"Last Sunday morning before the race, we all ate together as a team," she said. "Ned thinks it's a great way for us to bond before we go to war."

"We?"

She waved him off. "Honey, I'm the glue behind this team, the team mom. They'd be nothing without me."

Cal nodded. "Fair enough—go on."

"Well, everyone was there, except Burns. So, Ned sent someone to check on him in his room. He wasn't there either. We called his cell phone, too. Nothing. Then about halfway through breakfast, he showed up. Claimed he went for a run and got lost. He was sweatin' up a storm."

"And so you have proof that he snuck into the garage?"

"Not exactly, but it's a process of elimination. Everyone else was there."

Cal folded his arms and eyed her carefully. "What if someone snuck into the garage and sabotaged the car before breakfast? Did you ever think of that?"

"If they did, I would've seen 'em," she shot back. "I get up at five a.m. and park my butt down in the lobby and read the newspaper. It's my race day ritual. Nobody would've gotten out of there without seeing me."

"Does everybody know you do this?"

"Depends on if you get up early enough or not. The ones who are early risers have seen me down there before, I'm sure."

"So, they'd know to avoid you?"

"Exactly. And Owen Burns was one of those early risers."

"Could've been any of the other ones, too."

"Now, you're overthinking things. Don't you know that the simplest answer is often the right one?"

"This isn't a Hardy Boys novel."

"Well, you keep sniffin' around and you'll find out what I told you to be the truth."

"Okay," Cal said. "Thanks for the lead. I'll follow up on this and see what I can find out." He turned to walk away before stopping when she called out his name.

"Yes?" he answered.

"Keep my name out of this, okay? I know Ned doesn't want this story getting out, but we can't let a killer walk free—no matter what it might do to the integrity of Ned's team. Burns needs to go to jail."

***

CAL CALLED KELLY to see how she was doing as he headed toward the NASCAR hauler.

"Are you two having fun without me?" Cal asked once she answered.

"Not as much fun as we could be," she said.

"I wish I was there."

She laughed. "Don't lie, Cal. You're loving this stuff. I read your story. Just the kind of stuff you can't get away from."

"Okay, you got me. I'm enjoying this assignment, even if Folsom isn't."

She sighed. "No one ever trusts your instincts, do they?"

"You'd think some editor would start to trust me with my track record."

"Don't take it personally. They're just doing their job."

"And I'm doing mine. They don't always make it easy."

"Well, hang in there, honey."

Cal stopped and looked around while he talked. "I want to give you a heads up that I may need your help with some things here."

Her voice lightened. "Seriously?"

"I'm still trying to gather all the evidence so I can publish something more definitive, but I'll need to borrow your critical eye."

"That'd be a nice change of pace after changing diapers all day."

"Thanks, sweetie. You're amazing."

"Go get 'em—and be careful."

Cal hung up and entered the NASCAR hauler. He wasn't expecting a warm reception and braced himself for some pushback.

Cal knocked on the wall. "Mr. Simpson?"

Simpson stood up. "Well if it isn't the bur in my saddle, Cal Murphy." He reluctantly offered Cal his hand to shake.

Cal shook it and remained standing. "I know I'm probably not your favorite person right now, but—"

"You're just a notch above Osama Bin Laden right now in my book."

Cal put his hands up and hung his head. "I'm sorry if I've caused you any trouble, but I'm just doing my job."

"I didn't think your job consisted of rumors and innuendos."

Cal cocked his head. "Well, I'm here with a little more than that today."

"What'd ya mean?"

"I got the report back from Mrs. Tanner's independent investigator and he found the return spring was artificially stressed."

"And?"

"Well, first of all, you missed it—if that's true, of course. And secondly, it seems like somebody was trying to sabotage his car."

Simpson put his hands up and shook his head. "Now, I've already told you that you just can't go wandering around the garages messin' with cars whenever you want. As a result, I seriously doubt that's what happened."

"But if it did?"

"I'd be very careful about making any accusations."

"I've got several people lining up to tell me what happened, including an eye witness."

"I'd be leery of anyone making such proclamations, Mr. Murphy. This is a cut throat business and people will do anything to get ahead."

"Even falsely accusing someone else of murder."

"You'd be surprised."

"I promise to handle this wisely, but you must know I have to write about these findings. And I wanted to give you the courtesy of commenting on the findings." Cal pulled out a file and handed it to him.

Simpson sat back down and scanned the summary page before flipping through several other pages and looking at a couple of photos. Cal noted the glistening "Duke Dad" bumpersticker beneath his Tennessee paperweight. He then handed the file back to Cal.

"This definitely warrants another look by our investigators," Simpson said. "We are aware of the matter and will address it once we've had time to reopen an investigation."

"Thank you." Cal turned to leave.

"Wait," Simpson said. "When are you planning on writing about this?"

"Tomorrow's paper, tonight's blog."

Simpson sighed. "Is there any way you can hold off on this, at least for another week and a half until the season's over? I'd hate for something like this to overshadow some driver's championship season."

"I doubt that's possible. My editor wants this story now. I suggest you get out in front of it before it's all you're talking about for the next few days. I'm not interested in ruining your season, but somebody's dead—and it looks like it was murder. NASCAR didn't do this, but you sure as heck better not try to cover it up."

Cal exited the hauler and called Folsom.

"I've got a story for you, but I'm warning you that it's not going to be pretty. Get ready for some phone calls," Cal said.

"If it wasn't stirring the pot, where would the fun be in that?" he answered.

CHAPTER 22

RON PARKER GLANCED at his watch and tried to ignore the pain. If he was in the Phoenix area, at least he could tell his wife that he went for a hike and got bit then. It would bring plenty of questions, but none he couldn't answer creatively to assuage her concerns.

He checked his rearview mirror and wiped the sweat beading up on his forehead. Twenty more minutes until the nearest hospital.

I can make it.

Then he looked in his mirror again. Were his eyes playing tricks on him? He squeezed them shut and opened them again, squinting at the sight. The headlights of the car behind him seemed to be double. He repeated the process. Still double.

He felt like he might faint. He rolled all the windows down to get more air in the car and help him stay conscious.

That's when he felt a jolt.

What the—

Parker turned around to see the headlights from the SUV behind him just inches away from his car. He stomped on the gas, but to no avail. Another jolt.

The sweat started to pour off his forehead, stinging his

eyes. He took one hand off the steering wheel and tried to clear his face. He lurched forward again.

When he realized his escape tactic was failing, he decided to try something else. He started to veer into the other lane only to see another car there. The window was down on the passenger side and the man driving trained his gun on him. He motioned for Parker to pull over.

So this is how it ends? I don't think so.

Parker headed toward the shoulder and watched the two vehicles fall in line behind him and slow down. Then Parker slammed his foot on the gas and took off.

The nearest hospital was only two minutes away off the next exit. It'd take more explaining to do, but he preferred that to the obvious alternative.

However, he underestimated his assailants. Within seconds, they had boxed him in and forced him off the road.

Moments later, Parker staggered out of the car with his hands in the air.

One of the men swaggered up to him and jammed a 9 mm Glock into his chest. "Well, if it isn't Ron Parker. You're a hard man to find." He laughed and turned around to look at the three other men accompanying him. He stopped laughing and lunged back at Parker. "Where's my money?"

Parker cowered. "I'm going to have it for you tomorrow."

The man laughed. "Tomorrow? You think I'm stupid enough to fall for that Ronny boy? You've been running from us for quite a while. We blew it off for a while, but things are tight and it's time to collect. At least you quit making excuses." He grabbed Parker by the scruff of his neck and shoved him farther away from the highway shoulder.

"Please! I'm serious. I'm going to collect in the morning and get you your money, if I live."

The man grunted. "I was told to either get the money or extract a pound of flesh. It's bad for business if everyone thinks they can get away with stiffing us. Sometimes, it's worth fifty G's to send a message. You know what I'm sayin'?"

Parker started to wobble.

"Are you okay, man? You don't look too good," the man said before bursting out into laughter again.

Parker reached down to scratch his leg.

"Hey, now. Don't do anything stupid."

"It's a snake bite." Parker said, and slowly tugged on his pants leg to reveal a swollen calf. "I'm gonna die if I don't make it to the hospital in the next twenty minutes or so."

"You're makin' my job easy for me tonight." He turned toward the other three men. "Get him in the car."

Parker squirmed in protest, but he was so weak he could barely get out a word.

"One of you get his car. I love it when I can get my hands dirty without getting them dirty."

The man led the caravan back onto the Interstate toward Phoenix.

CHAPTER 23

CAL MADE HIS WAY through the mass of RVs covering a large swath of desert just below the Arizona foothills surrounding the raceway. While college football fans prided themselves on their pre-game tailgate, NASCAR fans made them look like they were hosting a 5-year-old's birthday party in comparison. Rotating spits dripped juice into fire pits. Country music blared over high-tech sound systems. Fans clinked beer bottles over toasts about their favorite drivers.

Now, this is a party.

And it stretched on for what seemed like miles to Cal.

He checked and rechecked his surroundings again to make sure he was going in the right direction.

Three blocks west of the store.

Cal looked behind him and counted. He'd gone two blocks since he came across Safeway's infamous tent grocery store.

One more to go.

He dodged fans whose parties had spilled out into RV city's main thoroughfare. One man bumped into Cal and nearly knocked him down. The man apologized and then offered Cal a beer.

"Thanks," Cal said as he took the man up on his offer.

"Who you think's gonna win this weekend?" the man asked.

"My money's on Cashman right now. That guy is driving lights out."

The man shot him a look. "You do realize what flag is flying over this RV right here, dontcha?"

Cal glanced upward to see a No. 39 flag waving in the light evening breeze. "Carson Tanner fans, I see."

"Dadgum right. That Cashman is trash, celebratin' like he did last week while Tanner was fightin' for his life just down the track. I wouldn't be surprised if Cashman was the one who sabotaged Tanner's car."

Cal chuckled. "Why would he do that when he could've just put him into the wall?"

"You gotta point," the man said as he nodded.

Cal held up the beer. "Thanks for the drink."

He continued on until he came to what looked like the RV at the location described by Ron Parker. No one was outside so he walked up the pair of steps and knocked on the door.

"Ron Parker? Are you there? It's me, Cal Murphy, the reporter from *The Observer*."

He stepped down and waited for a few moments. Nothing.

Just as he was about to leave, Cal noticed a light flicker on in the back of the RV. He spun back toward the door and waited.

Then he yelled again. "Mr. Parker, are you in there? It's me, Cal Murphy."

A few seconds later, the door unlatched and Mrs. Parker— at least who Cal hoped was Mrs. Parker—emerged, clothed in a bathrobe.

"Can I help you?" she asked.

"Yes, I'm supposed to meet Ron Parker. Is this his RV?"

She nodded. "I'm not sure where Ron is, but he's been gone for hours. I'm starting to get a little worried. He should've been back a long time ago. It's not like him to disappear like this." She stuck her hand out. "Nancy Parker. And you are?"

Cal offered his hand back. "Cal Murphy. I'm a reporter for *The Observer*."

"Oh, a reporter. What business do you have with Ron?"

"Not sure. He told me that he had something he wanted to show me. Have you tried calling him?"

"His phone just keeps going directly to voicemail."

"Would you mind giving me his number so I can try him?"

"Sure, just a minute." She disappeared inside the trailer to fetch her phone. When she returned, she read off the number for Cal.

She waited while he called it.

After half a minute, he shook his head. "Same thing. Straight to voicemail."

"He's a popular guy tonight," she said.

"Oh?"

"Yeah, this is the second time tonight people have come by looking for him. I gave his number to some other gentlemen who said they had a meeting set up with him for tonight."

"Who were they?"

"They didn't say."

"What'd they look like?"

"You sure ask a lot of questions."

Cal forced a smile. "I'm a reporter—that's what I do. If I somehow track him down before you do, I'll tell him you are wondering where he is."

She smiled. "I'd appreciate that. I'm really starting to get worried. And I'll do the same for you. Do you have a card?"

Cal handed her his card. "Tell him to give me a call once he gets back, if you see him first."

"Will do," she said as she closed the door.

Cal walked away and sighed. He knew something didn't add up.

Maybe Ron Parker had more damning information than I thought.

CHAPTER 24

EDDIE SIMPSON GRUMBLED as he walked through the garage area toward the media center at the Phoenix International Raceway. The report that Cal Murphy filed about Jessica Tanner's independent investigator's findings ruined his dinner. The higher ups suggested he quell the furor with a press conference. Handling the media wasn't part of his skill set. If it had been, there likely would not be a swarm of reporters standing outside the media center awaiting his arrival.

He lumbered along until he felt a sharp tug on his shirtsleeve. Turning to his right, he saw Ned Davis.

"Come here, Eddie," Davis said, pulling him toward his hauler.

Simpson shrugged him off. "I ain't got time for this, Ned. I've got a press conference in five minutes."

"It can't wait."

"It'll have to." He continued to rumble toward the media center.

Simpson arrived to find the building jammed with reporters and cameramen waiting to capture the event. Several media outlets were streaming the event live.

Simpson sighed as he opened the door and surveyed the scene.

Oh, brother.

Once he stepped up to the lectern, he arranged his papers and looked across the sea of faces. He'd dealt with most of these press members individually on at least one occasion—and he considered them all friends. They'd talk about their families, the demands of being on the road, sports, restaurants, movies. But at the moment, Simpson saw what looked like a pack of hungry wolves ready to shred him the second he opened his mouth.

Deep breath, Eddie. You can do this.

He cleared his throat and then spoke. "I have a prepared statement that I'm going to read before I take questions."

He shuffled the papers again and began reading.

"The entire NASCAR community was saddened at the passing of Carson Tanner last week at the Texas Motor Speedway. Everyone involved in this sport is aware of its inherent danger, which is why we work so hard to put safety first in everything we do.

"Our initial investigation into Carson Tanner's accident was that the throttle got stuck due to a faulty part, causing the unfortunate crash. Carson Tanner's widow, Jessica, sought permission to have a second look at the debris from the crash to determine if there was another explanation. Her investigator has claimed that the return spring on the throttle was artificially stressed with heat prior to the race.

"Our investigative team noted that part, but we determined that it was due to other race-related wear and tear on the spring. We will reopen our investigation at the request of Jessica Tanner and reexamine the part. We remain confident in our initial findings, but we recognize the importance of due diligence in this situation to allow us to close this tragic chapter in our sport's history with full knowledge of what actually happened."

Simpson drew a deep breath. He was about to take the first question when an aide tapped him on the shoulder and whispered something in his ear. Simpson's face fell, and everyone in the room noticed it.

"I'm sorry, but we're not going to be able to take any questions at this time. Something more pressing has come up," he said as he climbed down from the platform and raced toward the door.

A buzz filled the room as reporters looked quizzically at each other.

"This is bush league, Eddie," one of the reporters yelled at him.

Simpson stopped just short of the door. He turned around and stormed in the direction of the insult.

"Watch your mouth, son," Simpson said as he wagged his finger. "You have no idea what's going on."

"Exactly," the reporter said. "So, why don't you tell us?"

"I don't have all the details right now, but when I do, I'm sure someone from our press team will brief you." Simpson spun around and resumed his upstream trek through the sea of reporters blocking his way to the door.

"Seriously? That's it?" the reporter asked.

Simpson turned around. "The police just found someone dead on Rattlesnake Hill. There. You happy now?"

He hustled down the steps and muttered a string of expletives under his breath. This wasn't how the last few weeks of the NASCAR season were supposed to go. He didn't think there was any way it could possibly get worse than what happened a week ago in Texas. But somehow, it had.

CHAPTER 25

CAL HUSTLED TOWARD the impromptu press conference, not that he needed to. He already knew everything
Eddie Simpson was going to say—and he could gather the
filler quotes from the official NASCAR press release later in
the media center. But he wanted to see the action for himself.
He needed to see how Simpson handled himself in front of
the cameras.

But he never got the chance.

As he entered the gate to the media center, a host of
reporters and cameramen stormed out following Simpson.
They were shouting questions to him, but he waved them
off.

What did I miss?

He stepped back and watched the scene unfold. Reporters jammed their microphones in his face; other camera
crew members fought for the precious real estate over Simpson's head with their boom microphones. A flurry of questions asked simultaneously morphed into a cacophony of
shouting reporters. Simpson shoved a mic out of his face,
bit his lip, and marched on.

Cal grabbed a straggling reporter by the shirtsleeve.
"Hey, what happened in there?"

The reporter slowed down for a minute. "Eddie Simpson announced they're reopening the investigation into Carson Tanner's accident."

"That's what this buzz is all about?"

The reporter kept walking and shook his head. "The police just found a body up on Rattlesnake Hill."

Cal hustled after the man. "Did he say who?"

"No, not yet, but the police are investigating. The track's probably worried they won't be able to open for the rest of the races this weekend."

Cal thanked the reporter and stopped. He needed to climb the iconic hill and find out what was really going on. And, more importantly, who was dead.

His pace quickened as he left the pack of reporters hounding Simpson and headed for Rattlesnake Hill. He'd climbed the hill a couple of days before just to get a different perspective of the track and watch the sunset over the Arizona mountains surrounding the raceway. He thought it had to rank as one of the best natural features of any stadium in the country. A view from here allowed fans to see the entire track without any blind spots.

He trudged up the steep embankment devoid of any fans. At race time, fans would pack the hill with lawn chairs, coolers, and flags of their favorite drivers.

The tiered seating area for fans ended about three-fourths of the way up the hill, as it was topped with piles of large rocks and rattlesnake hideouts. The end of the seating area also marked the place where a Maricopa County Sheriff's deputy stood watch to provide a barrier between any snoopy members of the public and the officers investigating the scene.

Cal stopped about fifty yards short of the deputy when his phone buzzed. It was Folsom.

"What did I do this time?" Cal asked jokingly as he answered.

"You've written your last piece for *The Observer*, that's what," Folsom fired back.

"What? You're joking, right?"

"No, Cal, I'm not."

"What did I do? That story was tight yesterday."

Folsom sighed. "It has nothing to do with the story."

"What then? Why would you possibly fire me?"

"Maybe the fact that you ran up a five thousand dollar tab at a Phoenix strip club last night on strippers and bottles of Cristal."

"That's ridiculous. I did no such thing."

"Well, I've got pictures to prove it—along with credit card receipts."

"You've got to be joking. If this is some kind of sick joke, Folsom, it isn't funny."

"Nobody's laughing, Cal. Least of all, my boss."

Cal seethed as he turned toward the track and watched a few cars on practice runs. "I'm telling you right now, those pictures are fake. Someone must have stolen my credit card."

"Do you have it on you now?"

Cal looked into his wallet. "Yes."

"Then how did they steal it, genius?"

"I—I don't know, but somebody is messing with you."

"Cal, I told you when you started to go down this path to watch out. Bad things were gonna happen."

"You know I'm innocent, Folsom. You implied as much right there."

"What I know is that my publisher called me this morning with these photos and the alleged stories about what you were doing last night—and he believed what he saw."

"You can't believe everything you see."

"Or hear or read, right?"

"What are you suggesting?"

"Those are the lines we hear as journalists from anyone who's ever been caught in a lie. I wouldn't expect to hear any less from you."

"Come on, you know I'm being set up."

Folsom ignored Cal's pleas. "The good news for you is that the paper isn't going to press charges as long as you repay the five grand and change you rolled up last night."

"This is outrageous."

"Come home immediately, Cal, and get this taken care of so it doesn't cost you your career. I'll write you a recommendation, but we can't stand for this behavior. I'll forward you the pictures so you can see the evidence for yourself."

"I didn't do this, Folsom. You've gotta believe me. I wouldn't do this, especially not to Kelly. How do you think this makes me look now? If you fire me, it's gonna make it look like I did these things—and that'll crush her."

"Maybe you should have considered that before you went out clubbing last night."

Cal growled. "You're unbelievable, Folsom. You *know* me. You know I'd never do anything like that."

"If you're not back here on Monday with the money in hand, they're going to prosecute you."

"But—"

"Sorry, Cal. That's the way it is. I've gotta run."

Cal hung up and kicked at some loose rocks in front of

him. He took a deep breath and put his hands behind his head as he walked in circles for about a minute. This was not how he saw this day going, especially as he was on the verge of discovering who was behind Carson Tanner's death.

He remained pre-occupied with the stunning news and didn't notice the deputy who was just a few feet away.

"Is everything all right there, mister?" the deputy asked.

Cal spun toward the voice and stopped. He sighed. "Yes, everything's fine, sir. I'm just having a bit of a bad day."

"Well, it could be worse," the deputy said, nodding in the direction of the crime scene agents scouring the ground for clues.

Sensing an opportunity, Cal stopped his pity act. "What happened up there?"

The deputy shook his head. "Not sure, but a man's dead. Strange place to die if you ask me."

Cal froze as he heard some clicking noise. "Do you hear that?" The clicking continued.

"Just another rattlesnake."

"And you're not scared?"

The deputy patted his gun. "I feel pretty safe right now." He put his hand out. "Deputy Livingston."

Cal shook his hand. "Cal Murphy. Nice to meet you."

The pair stared down at the track below.

The deputy finally broke the silence. "So, what brings you up here today? Trying to get a peek at the dead?"

Cal shook his head. "Just needed to take a walk."

The deputy glanced down at Cal's media badge. "You sure it wasn't to find out what was going on up here?"

"Just wondering who it was—that's all."

"You think you might know the fellow?"

Cal took a deep breath. "Maybe. I was supposed to meet an informant last night and he never showed up. The people who were after him were dangerous."

"I see. Maybe we better talk more formally, Mr. Murphy?"

"Look, I don't wanna bother you any longer since I know you've got important work to do up here. I'm just gonna head on back to the track."

"If you know something, mister, you ought to tell us."

Cal looked at the ground and then back up at the deputy. He needed to study his eyes. "That's not a Mr. Ronald Parker up there, is it?"

The deputy immediately looked away, signaling to Cal that he was right.

"I'm not at liberty to discuss such things just yet until the next of kin has been notified," the deputy said. "Our spokesperson will be making a formal announcement later today. But I think perhaps we should definitely let you talk to some investigators now."

Cal started walking back down the hill. He turned and shouted over his shoulder. "Don't worry, Deputy Livingston, I'll be in touch very soon. But there's somewhere I've gotta go first."

CHAPTER 26

NED DAVIS STORMED into the NASCAR hauler, his face already beading with sweat despite the cool desert breeze.

"Where is he?" Davis yelled.

"Excuse me, sir," a young intern asked. She took a step back when she recognized him. "Who are you looking for?"

"Eddie Simpson. I need to talk to him right now," he growled.

"Follow me."

She led him back to Eddie's desk where he sat, head down staring at a folder.

"Eddie, someone's here to see you," she said before she scurried away.

"I told you it couldn't wait," Davis said.

Simpson didn't look up, pretending not to hear.

"Are you listening to me?" Davis asked.

Simpson waved him off and kept reading.

Davis reached into Simpson's cubicle and slammed the file shut before banging his fist on the desk. "We need to talk—now!"

Simpson stood up and looked around to see if any other employees were around. They weren't. He motioned for

Davis to sit. "Now, what can I help you with, Ned?"

"I know what's going on here," Davis started.

"I'm glad someone does. Would you please tell me?"

"Someone is trying to make it look like one of our guys sabotaged Carson Tanner's car last week."

Simpson grunted. "Tell me something I don't already know."

"So you think that, too?"

"I don't know what to think. I just know there are a lot of people gettin' up in my business and messing with things they shouldn't be messing with. We let that hack of an investigator take a look at everything at Jessica Tanner's request. It's not like we could refuse her. And of course he found something. It's all makin' my life a livin' hell."

"So, what are you going to do?"

"At this point, we've come to the conclusion that there's a strong possibility that some of the information that emerged from that report in *The Observer* is true."

"And what does that mean?"

"We're discussing the possibility of having you withdraw your car from the race so we can investigate your team."

"You can't do that. That's—"

Simpson held up his hand. "I know it sounds harsh, but our first priority is safety. And if you've got some guy on your team sabotaging your own car, who knows who might be next? You know we can't have this."

"That report is garbage."

"And you know this how? Can you account for everyone on your team the morning this alleged sabotage took place?"

"Absolutely. I ate breakfast with every one of them, just like I always do."

"As much as I'd like to take your word over this report, we need to do our due diligence here."

"So, you're gonna reopen the investigation?"

Simpson nodded.

Davis' eyes narrowed. "What are you gonna find?"

"Hopefully, the truth, so we can turn the focus back to racin'."

Davis poked Simpson in the chest. "No, that's not what you're gonna find."

"Hey, now. Knock it off, Ned."

Davis edged closer. "No, you listen to me. You're gonna find nothin' because nothin' happened. You understand?"

Simpson leaned back. "Just chill, Ned. If you guys didn't do anything wrong, you'll be fine."

"Not if the public already makes up its mind first—I'll be ruined. Nobody will come work for me."

"You can just clean house then."

"No, I can't. I've got too many guys under contract. It'd sink me if I had to start all over."

Simpson shook his head. "Come on, Ned. You expect me to believe that? Your team is flush with cash."

"Not like you might think. I just lost my star driver—and with him, all that sponsorship money."

"You'll get it back. Might take a year or two and you'll be winning championships before you know it."

"I don't have two years, Eddie."

Simpson cocked his head and furrowed his brow. "What do you mean?"

Davis gritted his teeth and lied. "I can't talk about it right now, but time is one thing I don't have."

"Aww, Ned. Quit playing games."

Davis shifted his weight from one foot to the other. "Didn't your daughter just get into Duke?"

Simpson shot him a look and stood up. "How'd you know that?"

Davis said nothing.

"Never mind. I've got work to do. So, if you'll excuse me."

Davis moved to impede Simpson's path. "I bet she was real excited about it, wasn't she? Probably her dream."

Simpson nodded and tried to sidestep Davis. "It was, but I've really gotta run."

"I've got a building named after me at Duke," Davis said. He eased out of the way and leaned in close to Simpson's ear. "I'd hate for her acceptance letter to be followed up with another letter that denied her entrance."

Simpson glared at him. "You wouldn't dare—"

Davis shook his head. "Of course not." He paused as Simpson started to walk away. But Davis wasn't finished with his thought. "As long as that investigation doesn't find anything."

Simpson glanced over his shoulder and shot another nasty look at Davis.

CHAPTER 27

OWEN BURNS STARED at the monitor just outside the Davis Motorsports hauler and let out a deep breath. He'd heard about the report from *The Observer* that Jessica Tanner's investigator found something that suggested foul play was involved in her husband's deadly crash. He nursed a cup of coffee in one hand, but it didn't seem to making his morning grumpiness vanish.

"Who calibrated this thing?" Burns yelled.

The rest of his team remained inside going over the schedule for the day. The only person outside was Alexa Jennings, who was stepping out of the hauler in time to hear him.

"Well, it wasn't me," she said.

Burns turned toward her and rolled his eyes.

Alexa walked up to him and stroked the back of his head. "Did somebody wake up on the wrong side of the bed?"

Burns grunted and withdrew.

She backed away before leaning on the chair next to his monitor. "Anything I can do to help?"

He stopped and glanced at her. "Maybe you can leave."

"Aren't we testy this morning?"

"I've got a lot on my plate today, so if you don't mind—"

"If you constantly find yourself in stressful situations, perhaps it's your own doing."

Burns closed his eyes and counted to five in his head. *God, please make her go away.* "You're the one adding to my stress right now."

"What? Worried they're going to find out you sabotaged your own team's car last week?"

Burns' eyes narrowed as he focused his gaze on her. "Now, you listen here. I put up with your crap all the time, but you're not going to come in here lobbing allegations like that. For all I know, you could've been the one to sabotage the car. So, don't start talking about things unless you know what you're talking about." He paused. "You're so clueless most of the time anyway."

She stamped her foot and put her hands on her hips. "I beg your pardon. I know more about what's going on here than you do. In fact, I know *exactly* what's going on with you, you little saboteur."

He stopped. "What are you talking about?"

"I know what happened. You were all upset about Carson's ineffectiveness on the track because it was making you look bad. He couldn't win a championship if his life depended on it—and little did he know, it really did."

He shook his head. "This is unbelievable."

She continued. "And then when you realized he was never going to live up to the lofty expectations you had for him—and that Ned wasn't in a position financially to fire him—you decided to take care of that yourself."

"What other delusional ideas are pinging around in that vast space between your ears?"

"Don't even try to deny it, Owen. I know the truth. And I know when you did it. And I've already told someone else about it—so don't even think about trying to kill me off to guarantee my silence."

"This is absurd. First of all, I'd never kill anyone. And second of all, I'd never do anything like you're suggesting, especially to Carson. He was one of the best drivers I've ever worked with and one of the best human beings I ever met. So, if you'll excuse me, I really need to get some work done here."

She remained undaunted. "Nice little speech, but I know the truth and have proof."

"Proof?" Burns started laughing. "You are crazier than you look—and that's sayin' somethin'. If you only knew half of what went on around here."

"I know everything that goes on around here, including when you snuck off to sabotage the car."

Burns rolled his eyes. "Oh, please, great oracle, tell me when I committed this crime."

"Don't mock me because it's my testimony that could ruin your career and send you away to prison for a long time."

"That's not an answer."

"Fine. It was at breakfast on Sunday morning. The whole team was there, but not you. You're the only one who was unaccounted for."

"What did you do? Check everyone's room key logs?"

"We had to send a search party out for you at breakfast. Even Ned was worried about you. He told me yesterday that he was ready to give you up to the investigators and tell them that you were suspiciously missing."

Burns waved her off. "Now, I know you're full of it."

"Why's that?"

"Because I was running an errand for Ned."

"Oh, really? What kind of errand?"

"The kind I don't talk about."

Alexa tied her hair up into a bun. "Typical. Nothin' but lies out of you. Good thing I told that reporter Cal Murphy about your actions that morning."

"You did what?"

"I told you I had to tell someone in case you decided to kill me next. That's my little insurance policy."

"You need to call him back right now and tell him the truth."

She giggled. "I already did."

"No, you didn't." He sighed. "You told him a story fabricated from your vivid imagination. Maybe you were still drunk from the night before or you just have it out for me, but I can assure you that you are dead wrong."

"Then tell me where you were?"

Burns looked at the ground. "I can't."

"You mean, you won't because you know how much trouble it'll get you in."

"No, I can't because I promised that I wouldn't."

"Fine. Play it that way. I'm going to let the entire press corps know about this at the next press conference I see taking place here."

"You can't do that, Alexa. I swear—"

"What? You swear you'll kill me?"

"No, you can't say that. You're going to get in big trouble for making up a story like that."

She threw her head back and laughed. "You always were a comedian."

Burns grabbed her by the arm. "Look at me, Alexa." He waited until she turned and stared him in the eyes. "I didn't do anything and you're only going to hurt yourself by making such accusations to the press."

"There's only one way to stop me," she said, pulling away from his grasp. "You tell me where you were and what you were doing."

"I can't. I promised."

She glared at him. "Break it—right now. Or else I'm going to crash the next media event."

Burns sighed. "Oh, what difference does it make? One way or another I'm screwed."

"Out with it." She folded her arms and eyed him closely.

"I was sneakin' out a woman for Ned."

She threw her hands in the air. "Now, I know you're lyin'."

He grabbed her arm again. "No, Alexa, I'm not. I can tell you her name and how to get in contact with her if you don't believe me. I've been doin' this for Ned long before you came around."

Her expression changed and she began to pace. "Why that no good lyin'—"

"Just calm down, Alexa. Going ballistic is only gonna make things worse."

"What can be worse than betrayal?"

Burns watched her walk back and forth, muttering to herself about how she should've known and how could she let herself fall for such a man. It went on for several minutes before he decided to intervene.

"There is something you could do," he said. "A little revenge, if you will."

She stopped and turned toward him. "And what's that?"

"I think he knows somebody on this crew sabotaged the car—and I think I know who it is. The last thing Ned wants is for that information to be confirmed. It doesn't look good on him or on the rest of this team. He's trying his best to keep it under wraps and out of the press."

"So, what can I do?"

"You can help me catch the saboteur."

"And how exactly am *I* gonna do that?"

"Sit tight. I've got a couple of ideas. If one of them doesn't work, I'm gonna need your help to pull it off."

CHAPTER 28

JESSICA TANNER BRUSHED the tears off her cheeks as she bore down on the road for the Phoenix International Raceway. The place she wanted to be was at a racetrack. Her doctor had warned her not to travel, but Jessica made a habit of going against the advice of others. It wasn't that long ago that her dad told her not to marry Carson or else he'd leave her heartbroken. She was sure he meant for some other reason, but in the end, her father was right.

Speak of the devil.

Jessica's phone buzzed and her father's face filled the screen, identifying him as the caller.

"Hi, Dad."

"Hey, sweetie. Where are you? I'm outside your house. Wasn't I supposed to come over today to help paint the baby's room?"

Oh, shoot.

"Sorry, Dad. I totally forgot about that."

"Where are you? I can wait—or just use the hidden key."

"Go ahead and use the key."

"When are you gonna be back?"

"Not for a while?"

"Like later this afternoon or this evening?"

"Maybe Monday."

"Monday? Where'd you go?"

"Phoenix." She cringed and braced for the fallout.

"What are you doing in Phoenix?" he asked, incredulous.

"I've got some business to take care of, Dad."

"What kind of business?"

"I need people to find out about what caused Carson's death."

"Oh, honey, don't do that. You're pregnant. You should be home resting."

"But, Dad, if I don't, I may lose my chance to prove that Carson's death was no accident. I need people to hear me—and believe me."

"Look, I know you're stressed about money now, but we'll help you. Whatever you need, we'll take care of it."

"Will you take care of the half-million dollar surgery my baby needs?"

"What?"

"Yeah, you heard me—a half-million dollars. My health insurance is refusing to cover the procedure, claiming it's elective."

"But—"

"Meanwhile, I've got a life insurance company that doesn't believe my husband was murdered. At this point, if I don't look out for myself, no one will."

"Jessica, it's not worth the stress."

"Yes, it is. But don't worry about me. I'll be fine. Just make my life less stressful by doing a good job on the baby room, okay?"

"Jessica, I—"

Her phone beeped.

"Sorry, Dad, I've got another call coming in. Gotta grab this. I'll be in touch."

She switched to the other line with the swipe of her finger. "Hello."

"Jessica Carson?"

"Yes?"

"Your late husband owed us a half million dollars in gambling debts."

"He what? Who is this?"

"You have one week to wire us the money. I will text you instructions. Don't be late."

"This is a sick joke."

"This is no joke. One week, Jessica. You have one week."

The caller hung up.

Jessica screamed and clenched her fists as the race track came into full view.

She felt the baby kick. And then she started to hyperventilate.

Just take a deep breath and relax.

She pulled into the parking lot to pick up her pit pass and got out of her car. After two steps, her knees weakened and she started to feel faint.

She sat down on the ground and tried to slow her breathing.

One of the track workers noticed her and ran to her side. "Are you all right, lady?"

Jessica held up her right index finger. "I'll be just fine." She tried to get up.

"Here, let me help you," the worker said as he bent over and steadied her arm.

"No, I'm fine. I can do this."

Then Jessica collapsed onto the ground and went limp.

"Someone call 9-1-1," the worker shouted.

CHAPTER 29

CAL SWALLOWED HARD before dialing Kelly's number. If investigative journalism taught him one thing it was that secrets had a funny way of getting out. He took that knowledge and applied it to his marriage, attempting to be forthright in every encounter. He learned that some situations required him to act more judiciously when revealing the truth, yet the truth must be presented in some semblance or another. In this instance, he couldn't think of any way to gently break the news that he'd been fired—and the alleged reason for it.

"Hey, you! I was just thinkin' about you. I was making out a menu for next week and I've got your favorite planned for Monday night when you get back. How are things going in the hunt for the saboteur?"

"Well, you might want to make that meal earlier."

"Why's that? What happened? Are you coming home today?" The excitement in her voice leaked out.

"Maybe. But it's nothing to be happy about it."

"Why's that?"

Cal took a deep breath. "Folsom fired me this morning."

"Fired you? Are you kidding me? What in the world for? Budget cuts? Pressure from advertisers?"

"I wish. Something far worse."

"Worse? What happened? What did you do?"

"It's not what I did, but what they *think* I did."

"And what's that?"

"Someone sent some anonymous pictures to Folsom of me at a strip club here in Phoenix along with receipts showing that I racked up a large tab on the company card."

"Cal! How could you?"

"No, no, no. Now listen to me. I didn't do it. Someone framed me. The pictures were Photoshopped. I never even went to a strip club. You know I wouldn't do that."

Silence.

Cal took a deep breath. "You've gotta believe me. I'd never do that to you, much less think about using the company credit card to do that. I'm not stupid."

Still silence.

"Come on, Kelly. Say something. You believe me, right?"

After another pause, she finally answered. "I wanna believe you, Cal. It's just that—"

"It's just that what? You think I'd actually do something like that."

"If the story led you there, I think you'd do whatever it took."

"Kelly, come on. Think rationally. The last place I'd ever get credible information is at a strip club. And in the interest of full disclosure, last night I wrote a story and then went to the track to meet a contact. I spent some time with an elderly woman whose husband was missing only to find out this morning that he was dead on a hillside."

"Hmmm. Sounds like you."

"Of course, it is. I didn't do this. In fact, I want you to

prove it for me."

"And how can I do that?"

"Utilize your photography skills and examine the photos. Highlight how they were Photoshopped and send them to Folsom."

"He sent you the pictures?"

"Folsom wanted to prove to me that he had them. But I must warn you, it's pretty horrific. I'm tempted to get someone else to do it because I don't want to even put the idea in your head that I did these things."

"Don't worry. I'll purge the mere idea if I can prove you're telling the truth."

"Seriously? You still doubt me."

"I guess I believe you. That's not your style."

"Thank you. I'm going to send you the photos now."

"Okay. I'll let you know once I'm able to prove it."

"I love you. You gotta know I'd never do something like that and hurt you—much less risk my job over it."

"I know. Be safe."

Cal hung up and let out a long breath.

That was worse than telling my brother I wrecked his Mustang.

He looked at the ground and rubbed his face, contemplating his next steps: Keep following leads in order to uncover the saboteur or go home and let Folsom deal with the consequences of missing out on a big story because he believed some fake photos. The second option was vengeful, and one he wanted to choose so he could stick it to his weak-kneed editor. But that would mean letting someone get away with something—or at least letting another reporter beat him to the punch. And he would never let that happen, except under the most extraordinary of circumstances. Cal didn't count losing his job as that extraordinary.

While he was thinking about where to go and who to talk to, a voice snapped him out of his mental deliberations.

"Rough morning?" the man asked.

"Not as rough as riding bareback without chaps," Cal quipped.

The man offered his hand and forced a smile. "Burt Glover, chaplain for Pro Racers of America."

"Nice to meet you. I'm Cal Murphy, a reporter for *The Observer*."

"Well, Cal, you look like you could use some coffee."

Cal shook his head. "I look that bad, huh?"

"I've seen worse, but I know what a bad-morning face looks like."

"You don't know the half of it."

Glover, who was already holding a mug, gestured for Cal to follow him toward his hauler. "You can tell me all about it on the way."

Cal nodded and fell into lockstep with Glover.

"So, what terrible hand did life deal you this morning?"

"I am about to break a major story and I got a call from my editor telling me I'd been fired."

"What would make him do that?"

"Someone who doesn't like the story I'm working on made it look like I ran up a big bill on the company credit card at a place I shouldn't have been."

"Casino? Strip club?"

Cal nodded. "The second one." He paused. "But I didn't go. Someone created fake photos of me, making it look like I was there. And they also stole my credit card number and ran up a huge bill."

They arrived at the hauler. Cal followed Glover inside where a pot of hot coffee awaited.

"Have a seat," Glover said. He topped off his mug and poured a cup for Cal.

They both sat down and took a few sips before continuing.

Glover studied Cal. "So, what are you gonna do now?"

"I'm gonna finish what I started, with or without a paper."

"Good for you."

"It's the only thing I know how to do."

Glover leaned back in his seat. "Well, don't get too discouraged by all this. You're in good company."

"What do you mean?"

"The Bible is full of stories about men who were unjustly accused. My personal favorite is Joseph."

"What happened to him?"

"If you're on a deadline, I don't have enough time. But the long and the short of it is he was a slave who was accused of sexually assaulting his owner's wife. Then he went to prison."

Cal sighed. "Sounds promising."

"That wasn't the end. Joseph eventually became the second in command of Egypt."

"Now, I can get behind that."

"Just a little encouragement for you. Things might be bad for a while, but just keep doing the right thing and eventually the truth will come out."

"Don't I know that. It's my job to make sure the truth always comes out."

Glover stood up and shook Cal's hand. "Thanks for stopping by."

Cal raised his cup. "Thanks for the coffee."

"Anytime. And you know where to find me if you need to talk again."

Cal smiled and slipped outside the hauler. He assessed the scene again. The garage area bustled with activity. Car engines roared as technicians tinkered with settings. Reporters interviewed drivers. Fans zipped around taking photos of their favorite driver's car and hoped for a photo op. Everything looked normal.

Almost everything.

He glanced over his shoulder to notice two guys who appeared out of place. They looked like they belonged to a security detail. Their attempts to blend into the background only made them stick out to Cal. Dark suits, dark glasses, alone. They both appeared to be staring out into space as if they were looking over the crowd.

Cal wondered who they were, but he didn't want them to realize he'd noticed them. So he walked casually for about fifty yards before he stopped. He pulled out his cell phone and began to have a fake conversation. As he scanned the area, he saw the men had moved closer toward him.

Are they following me?

Cal kept walking, his pace quickening along with his heart rate. He walked around the corner of the garage office and hustled near a stack of tires. In a matter of seconds, the men appeared. They looked frazzled as if they'd lost something—or someone.

Cal stood up in plain sight and glanced around again. This time, they were looking right at him. He had no idea who they were, but he knew who they were after.

He no longer had the chance to mull his next move in his investigation, forced to do the only thing he could do—run.

CHAPTER 30

OWEN BURNS PICKED the cheese off his sub sandwich and laid it on top of the wrapper. He cursed under his breath and felt his blood pressure rise.

How many times do I have to tell them …

Jackson Holmes sauntered up and gawked for a moment at Burns' antics. He finally broke his silence, alerting Burns to his presence.

"You tryin' to catch a rat?" Holmes asked.

Burns didn't look up. "Haven't you heard? Rats don't like cheese. They like peanut butter." He paused. "But I use other methods to catch rats."

"Oh? Do tell."

"I like to let them run loose for a while and then—BAM!" Burns clapped his hands. "I put them in a trap they can't escape."

Holmes furrowed his brow. "Sounds like a regular rat trap to me."

"That's what they all think, but it's the one behind them that they need to be on the lookout for."

"I'll remember that if I'm ever looking for something to eat at your house."

Burns laughed. He gestured toward a tray of subs. "You

better get yourself something to eat. Got a big afternoon ahead of us."

Holmes grabbed a sandwich and disappeared.

After reassembling his sandwich sans cheese, Burns stood up and turned around to watch the garage activity.

Another day, another dollar.

He sat down and continued eating only to turn around when he heard approaching footsteps. It was Dirt. Burns turned back around and didn't saying anything.

"What's got your goat today?" Dirt asked.

"Tryin' to figure out who on my crew sabotaged Tanner's car last week."

Dirt sighed and rolled his eyes. "Oh, great. This again, huh? You seriously believe all those reports in the news? Those people are just tryin' to sell a story."

Burns stood up. "Or maybe you're just tryin' to cover it up?"

Dirt put his hands out and motioned for Burns to sit down. "Settle down, old man. If that report is true, I can assure you I had nothing to do with it. You know my hands are clean."

"Says the man known as Dirt."

Dirt edged closer. "They don't call me Dirt because of what's underneath my fingernails."

"Please tell me how you got your nickname then," Burns said, sarcasm dripping in his tone.

"Keep accusin' me and you'll figure it out soon enough."

"What's that supposed to mean?"

"You keep tryin' to pin this on me and I'll tell everybody what happened when you went into debt fifteen years ago and why Greg Grant really lost that race in Homestead."

Burns' eyes narrowed. "What are you talkin' about?"

"Don't play dumb with me. You know exactly what I'm talkin' about."

"You're dumber than you look if you'd believe such a story."

Dirt let out a short breath. "Believe it? I heard it from your own mouth one night. You had a little too much in you and you were shootin' off about it."

Burns waved dismissively and turned around. "You're full of it now."

"The hell I am—I've even got a recording of it. One I'm holding on to in case you lose your entire mind and start blamin' this on me in the press."

"I'm callin' your bluff."

"Oh, so, you didn't lose a couple hundred grand gambling? And you didn't repay your debt by tweakin' Grant's car so it was so tight that it wasn't competitive in the final race of the season—a race he only needed to finish twenty-fifth in to win the cup that year? You didn't do that?"

Burns' shoulders slumped and he stared at his plate.

"That look says it all," Dirt snapped.

Burns looked up. "That wasn't all there was to the story. I only did it because I needed some money to care for my momma. They were gonna put her in an institution if I didn't come up with a deposit."

"Cry me a river. You were more worried about someone crushing your knee caps than you were your momma."

Burns stood up and lunged toward Dirt. "Don't you ever talk about my momma—God rest her soul."

Dirt backed up. "I promise to keep her name out of my mouth if you do the same to keep my name out of yours when you go slingin' these accusations around. Got it?"

Burns nodded and sat back down. He gritted his teeth and cursed under his breath.

Dirt started to walk away and then stopped. "I'll be watchin' you tomorrow, Burns."

CHAPTER 31

BEARING A BOUQUET, Ned Davis knocked on the hospital door to Jessica Tanner's room. He conjured up his best sympathetic face and hoped she would buy it. While he felt a loss for her husband, he couldn't say he was sad to see her go with him—only she hadn't exactly gone yet. He loathed her meddlesome ways with Carson while he was a driver, and he detested them even more so now.

He forced a smile and plodded toward her bedside. "How are you feeling?"

Jessica scooted up and pushed a button on the automatic bed to help her sit more upright. She rubbed her belly and looked down. "I've been better."

"I brought you something," he said, offering the flowers.

"Thanks. Can you put them over there?"

He nodded and set them on a bedside table. "What are the doctors saying about what happened? I came as soon as I heard."

"That was kind of you, Mr. Davis. I've been under a lot of stress over the last week and I think it just started to take its toll on my body."

"I wanted to stop by with a get well wish and see what I could do to help."

Jessica sighed. "You know, Mr. Davis, I don't think there's much you can do, other than help NASCAR come to the same conclusion as my independent investigator did. Help them figure out who tampered with Carson's car. It'll give me some peace, as well as help me get the life insurance I so desperately need."

"I can help with money if you need it."

"It's not about money for me, to be honest. I've got some unexpected bills I need to pay. But even more so, it's more about her," she said as she pointed at her stomach. "I found out my baby needs costly surgery before she's born. He's got a condition that requires open womb surgery."

"Oh, wow. I'm sorry to hear that."

"Yeah, it really sucks." She paused. "But we're gonna make it."

"Well, I can help pay your medical bills and give you a generous bereavement package."

"That'd be kind of you."

"How does five hundred thousand dollars sound?"

"What's the catch?"

"No catch—just walk away from this investigation. It's important for you right now to put it all behind you and move on."

Jessica's eyes narrowed. "Move on? My husband died in one of your cars and you're not the least bit curious as to how something like that happened—and you just want me to move on? What kind of person are you?"

"I'm trying to help you."

"Help me? By paying me off?"

"That's not what I'm saying. I'm—"

"No, you listen to me," Jessica said, wagging her finger.

"I know exactly what you're up to. Whether you're trying to protect yourself or your brand or somebody on your team, I don't know. But what I do know is that I'm not moving on until I find out what happened last week. Or more importantly, who sabotaged Carson's car. Is that clear?"

"Jessica, I'm afraid you're making a big mistake. They're not going to find anything because there's nothing to be found."

The steady beat reported by Jessica's heart monitor quickened. "I'm sure you're going to make sure that's the case, aren't you?"

"I hope you're not trying to suggest that I can control NASCAR, because let me assure you that no one can. I want the truth too, but the truth is it was an accident. And anything else that continues to challenge those findings does nothing but weaken our team and our brand."

"I knew it. That's all you care about is that stupid race team of yours and your sacred brand and marketing opportunities. You don't care that one of the greatest men I've ever known died in one of *your* cars less than a week ago. And here you are with the gall to try to buy my silence."

Davis chuckled. "One of the greatest men you've ever known? You need to get out some, Jessica. He wasn't who you thought he was."

"I lived with him. I know what kind of man he was. And you better watch your mouth."

"Did he tell you about his gambling debts?"

Jessica didn't flinch.

"Oh, so you knew. Did he tell you how much he owed? Because I can tell you that it was a lot. He used to get visits from some guys that I had to get extra security for because they roughed him up one night."

She put her hands over her ears. "Enough. Get out, now!"

Davis started walking backward toward the door. "What? I thought you were determined to get the truth out? Maybe it'll all come out. Who knows?"

Jessica picked up a bottle of orange juice next to her beside and flung it at Davis. He slipped out just before it crashed against the door.

He took a deep breath and strode down the hall.

Nobody turns down my money. Nobody.

CHAPTER 32

CAL WIPED THE SWEAT streaming down his face off with his sleeve and peeked over his shoulder. The two men remained in full pursuit, eyes locked on him. Cal sprinted toward a tram stop where a tram began its departure.

Another truck pulled out in front of the tram, causing a slight delay. It was the break Cal needed. He hurdled the chain latched across the left side of the tram that served as a minor safety device—and slid into his seat. The conductor scowled but said nothing as the tram began moving forward.

Cal glanced over his shoulder. The two men continued racing toward the tram.

"Friends of yours?" the conductor in the back asked as he observed Cal's nervous looks at the fast-approaching men.

Cal shrugged and returned his gaze forward.

The tram rolled down a hill and under the track, headed for the next stop outside the raceway entrance.

As the tram approached the next stop, Cal didn't wait for it to stop moving. He leaped over the chain and landed on his feet. He shot a quick look behind him and saw the two men still in pursuit.

Cal navigated the congested area outside the stadium.

Fans had begun to arrive for the Xfinity Series race early that afternoon. They awaited entrance to the stadium, moving like a listless tide. It created a challenging obstacle for Cal.

He pushed his way through as efficiently—and as politely—as possible. He knew the fun-going crowd could transform into a mob in seconds if he knocked over a small child or an elderly lady. When he broke into a small clearing, he looked behind him to see the men peering above the crowd, scanning for him.

Cal continued to head for a walkway that served as a safe perimeter for fans to circumnavigate the stadium. However, it was fenced in on both sides almost the entire way around, devoid of almost any getaway exits for over a half-mile. But it was the only way Cal saw to maintain his lead and avoid attracting unwanted attention.

"Cal Murphy! You look like you need a pair of sneakers and gym shorts movin' like that."

Cal turned to his right in the direction of the airy voice with a Southern twang. It was Alayna French, sitting in a golf cart with one of her corporate sponsors.

"Hi, Alayna. What are you doing out here?" Cal asked as he looked over his shoulders at the two men closing in.

"We're goin' to the pre-race concert. Need a lift?"

Cal jumped into the seat. "I thought you'd never ask."

Alayna launched into full promotion mode, jamming nearly every corporate sponsor that supported her driver into a quick description of what she was doing that day. Cal sensed she was fishing for a commitment to show up for at least one of the events. He tried to act interested despite focusing on the men who hadn't stopped running after him.

"They never quit, do they?" he muttered under his breath.

Alayna stopped. "What was that? You'll be there after the race? Is that what you said?"

"Yeah, yeah," Cal answered. "Sounds good. Can you let me out here? I'll see you then."

The driver slowed down and Cal jumped out and headed straight for RV city. If ever there was a place to get lost, this was it.

As he peered over the rise, RVs and campers covered what seemed like at least a couple hundred acres. He hustled toward the entrance, checking over his shoulder once more to notice the men no more than a couple hundred yards away.

He disappeared into RV city and began to search for a more permanent place to hide. With a few moments to catch his breath, Cal thought a clearer mind might help him plot a way back unharmed. He'd been so focused on escaping that he hadn't thought to look for an officer. He decided that if he could find a location to hide in for a few hours, he could re-emerge and alert the on-site law enforcement to what was happening. It was the best plan he could think of on the fly.

Cal scooted down one makeshift street, sliding between a pair of RVs to the next street at every opportunity. While the area made it easy to disappear, the wide alleys between each row of RVs made it easy to search for someone. If he didn't switch often enough, they'd be on him again—and he might not get so fortunate in his attempts to escape.

As he dashed down one street and aimed to switch to another, he ran past a couple, grilling out and drinking beer.

"Where do you think you're goin' so fast, young man?" the man grumbled. "Don't just cut through my RV without stopping to have a drink."

Cal noticed a vehicle was parked in the passageway between the two RVs and he couldn't pass through them. He froze and turned around. The old man grinned. He had a beer bottle extended in one hand and a pair of tongs in the other.

"Sit for a spell," the man said. "You should never be in a hurry around here, much less empty handed. I thought I was gonna have to call the cops if you didn't stop."

Cal eased back toward the couple. He hustled toward them and then glanced in both directions down the street. Then he surveyed the RV site. The flags hanging off the RV provided a good cover, which was why Cal hadn't noticed the couple in the first place.

He decided to take the man up on his offer.

"Cal Murphy," he said, extending his hand.

"I'm Fred and this is Norma," the man said, gesturing toward his wife. She rocked in her chair and smiled at Cal. Fred put a beer in Cal's hand.

"Thanks," Cal said.

"So, where you off to in such a hurry? The race is *that* way."

"Long story—and to be honest, I don't have much time."

"I must admit, you look kinda suspicious running around like that. I figured I'd kill you with kindness."

Cal laughed. "I don't get much of that in my line of work."

"You a politician?"

Cal laughed again. "No, a journalist."

The man reached his hand out and leaned toward Cal. "Then give me that beer back." His straight-man comedy routine left Cal laughing. Fred then broke out into a smile and sat back down.

"So, who's gonna win the race?" Fred asked.

Before Cal could answer, he looked up to see the two men staring right at him. "Sorry, gotta run. Now's the time to call the cops!"

Cal leaped out of his chair and hit his full stride in less than three seconds. He had about a fifty-yard lead on the two men, but they were closing fast.

Cal dashed down one street and then found two RVs to cut through to the next one. He weaved his way back toward the throngs headed for the stadium. Down one street and through another. Back and forth. His attempts to lose them seemed to fail at every turn.

However, it did give him enough time to scout out a location to hide. He noticed one RV two streets back that had set up a temporary brown lattice around the bottom of the vehicle. And no one was there.

Cal worked his way back toward the RV and lost the men, giving him just enough time to move a piece of the lattice to the side so he could slither in behind it. Everything about it was perfect. It was dark and kept everything under the RV hidden.

With his face pressed to the gravel pad beneath the RV, he watched and waited. He looked at his watch. The race started in an hour and there would be another wave of latecomers in about thirty minutes. He thought he could blend in with that crowd long enough to find a sheriff's deputy to help him.

Cal scanned the area and saw very little activity, with the exception of a small group of fans wandering toward the stadium. The smell of a nearby barbecue wafted across Cal's nose, while a George Strait song blared over the loudspeaker several RVs away.

Why would you ever leave and go to the race?

Cal thought it was heaven.

Until a pair of shiny black shoes appeared in front of the lattice.

Cal froze. So did the shoes.

For several agonizing seconds, Cal held his breath and hoped those shoes didn't belong to whom he thought they did.

Without warning, the man squatted down and peered through the latticework.

"Hello there, Mr. Murphy."

Cal rolled toward the other side and kicked the lattice out. He scrambled to his feet, only to be met by the other man.

"We need to talk." The man recoiled and punched Cal in the face.

Cal slumped to the ground.

CHAPTER 33

OWEN BURNS CONCLUDED that the only way to beat a cover up was to produce indisputable evidence. And the evidence was there, right in front of him—if he could just get his hands on it. If NASCAR had truly suspected foul play in Carson Tanner's accident, they would have confiscated the car indefinitely. Or if the police had been involved, the footage would be airing on the cable news cycle for the next week and a half. But when Ned Davis had everyone in his hip pocket, people only looked for what he wanted them to find.

He drove back to his hotel with Jackson Holmes to drop off a few things before going to an early evening dinner.

"You all right, Burns?" Holmes asked.

He shrugged. "I've been better."

"Well, we just haven't had a chance to really talk about what happened to Tanner."

"What's there to talk about? It sobers us up and reminds us that none of us are immortal. But I can't see getting into a deep conversation about it. Why? Do *you* need to talk about it?"

"He was a good guy and I miss him."

Burns sighed. "We all do. He went far too soon. But he wasn't perfect."

"Nobody's perfect. He was far from it."

"Oh?"

"Yeah, all those gambling debts he racked up."

Burns laughed. "Who doesn't have gambling debts these days?"

Holmes remained stoic. "I don't."

"Well, congratulations."

"And I've never run anyone over in a race car."

Burns shot Holmes a look. "That was a long time ago—and completely accidental."

"Maybe. You never know about people."

"True, but most people can't hide that kind of darkness forever. Eventually, it comes out."

"You think people will ever find out what kind of person Carson Tanner really was?"

Burns shook his head. "He was normal—deeply flawed but loving and kind. He did his best and that's all you can ask for."

"And he left his daughter fatherless and his wife a widow."

Burns glanced at Holmes and sighed. "Are you sure you didn't have anything against Tanner? You sure sound like you don't have a lot of compassion right now."

"Rough week."

"Tell me about it." Burns reached for his door handle. "I'll be right back."

Burns hustled into the hotel with his bag. He was rounding the corner toward his room when he nearly ran over Todd Cashman, who was engrossed with texting someone.

"Whoa there, big fella. Is there a fire down the hall?" Cashman asked after the collision.

"Sorry, Cashman. Just wasn't paying attention."

Cashman broke into a wry smile. "I hope you're paying more attention tomorrow when I school your young driver on the ins and outs of big league driving. This ain't the kiddie circuit."

"Oh, we'll be ready. Don't you worry."

"So will I, but that's probably a shock to you since you think I don't prepare like a real racecar driver."

Burns was taken aback by the accusation. "What are you talkin' about?"

"Oh, that little article in *Racing Weekly* a few months back. I read it all right. You said that Cashman's having a good year, but it's due to the fact that he's avoided any of the major accidents that have taken out race teams this season and not because he's more prepared than everyone else."

"Hey, that was taken out of context. That's not what I meant."

Cashman nodded. "Fair enough, tubby. We'll find out who's done their homework tomorrow. I'm afraid you'll be disappointed after I leave winner's circle drenched in champagne and coated with confetti."

Burns held his tongue, wondering if this was the moment to broach the subject he needed to talk to Cashman about.

Screw it. I'm going for it.

"Look, Cashman. I know we've had our moments over the years, but I do have a favor to ask of you."

"A favor?" Cashman pointed at his own chest. "From *me*?"

Burns let out a long breath. "Yeah. And you're the only one who can help me."

"How's that?"

"If I recall correctly, in Texas your hauler was set up with a clear view of the garage across from our car."

"Yeah. So?"

"And your hauler is rigged with a security surveillance system, right?"

Cashman furrowed his brow and tapped his foot. "What are you gettin' at, Burns?"

"I'm sure you've heard the rumors that someone supposedly sabotaged Tanner's car last week. And if the story I've heard is true, whoever fiddled with the return spring that caused the accident would be on your security video feed."

"*You* want me to give you *my* security tapes?"

Burns nodded.

"Are you crazy?"

"Come on, Cashman. What's it gonna hurt?"

"My reputation, for one. Everybody's gonna say that the only reason I'm in the championship race is because someone sabotaged Carson Tanner's car. And then how do I know you won't try to tie your little weasel to me?"

"You know we'd never do that. We've got enough problems of our own."

Cashman chuckled. "You sure do. That starts with tryin' to figure out how to beat me tomorrow." He jabbed his finger into Burns' chest. "Better bring your A game, loser."

Cashman spun and walked away.

"Really? You're just gonna walk away like that?"

Cashman raised his fist in the air defiantly, refusing to turn around as he continued down the hall. "I'm not gonna taint my title, porky."

Burns seethed. "You're not gonna win one either, punk."

Burns took a deep breath. Convincing Cashman to give up the tape was the easiest path to revealing the saboteur—if there truly was one.

Guess I'll have to do it the hard way.

CHAPTER 34

CAL REAWOKE IN THE TRUNK of a car bounding over rises and bottoming out in large holes. Whoever had taken him held no regard for his personal comfort. A jack jabbed him in the back every time the car sank into a depression over the rocky terrain. He could tell it was still light outside through the porous holes in the trunk, but he couldn't guess what time it was—or if it was even still Saturday. He hoped it was, but that was far down on his list of wishes at the moment. He wouldn't care what day it was if he could escape the thugs holding him hostage.

Since he'd already failed to elude his assailants, he chose to shift his mental energy toward figuring out where he was. Faint traces of dust leaked into the trunk through the various holes. From the sound of the tires, Cal deduced they were traveling on a poorly kept dirt road—if it was even a road at all. His exercise did little to help him deduce his location.

After another fifteen minutes, the brakes squealed as the vehicle lurched forward and came to a stop.

Finally!

Cal heard two doors open and slam shut before the rattling of keys gave way to a mechanical click. The trunk flew open, revealing a dusky Arizona evening. Cal tried to climb out before one of the men yanked him out with one hand and slung him to the ground.

"Get up," the man snapped.

Cal rose to his feet slowly, dusting off the dirt that caked his clothes.

"I'm gonna make this simple for you," the man said as he opened up a laptop computer. "Look at this."

Cal's jaw dropped as he stared at the image on the screen.

"Recognize her?"

Cal nodded. It was Kelly.

"This is a live feed—and I'm sure you wouldn't want anything to happen to your dear wife, would you?"

Cal glared at the man. "Leave her out of this. She had nothing to do with anything. Just tell me what you want."

"We want you to get on a plane and go home, never to show your face around a racetrack again. Got it?"

"What did I do?" Cal asked.

"I think you know exactly what you've done. And it's time for you to leave."

Cal didn't flinch. "Who are you working for?"

The man pulled out his gun and jammed it underneath Cal's throat. "I ask the questions around here now. It's time for you to go." He whipped Cal in the head with the butt of his gun while the other man put a sack on Cal's head and heaved him back into the trunk.

***

AN HOUR LATER, Cal awoke in his own car to a black sky. On the passenger seat was a ticket for a flight home, scheduled to depart in ninety minutes.

He reached for his phone. As he was dialing, a text message appeared on his screen:

We're watching you.

Cal glanced around in every direction, searching for whoever might be watching him. Then he saw a pair of headlights flash at him.

Great.

Instead of calling Kelly, he decided to text her. At best, they'd bugged his car. At worst, his phone. He had to take a chance on getting in touch with her somehow.

He started to type when another message flashed up on his screen.

Quit texting and drive ... or we'll make your life miserable again.

Cal put down his phone and fired up the engine. He eased onto the accelerator and headed toward the airport.

A pair of headlights on high beams glared in his rearview mirror.

CHAPTER 35

JESSICA TANNER TRIED to take a deep breath but failed. With each passing second, she recognized the necessity to do so, even without the nurse's constant reminders. After a minute, she succeeded and leaned back in her bed."

I need to call Cal.

She picked up her phone and started dialing his number.

A nurse entered the room and rushed over to her bedside. "I don't think that's such a good idea, Mrs. Tanner. You need to rest," she said as she wrangled the phone away from Jessica. "You can call people later."

Jessica sat up. "How dare you? I need to make a phone call right now. You can't tell me what—"

Jessica's vitals spiked as she turned her focus on trying to regain control of her breathing. No sooner had she stopped hyperventilating than her face contorted and she began to grunt.

"This is why you need to listen to me," the nurse said, seizing control of the phone from Jessica's limp hand. She put the phone on Jessica's bedside table.

"I think I'm—I'm having a contraction," Jessica stammered.

"Sure you are." The nurse fluffed up Jessica's pillows and propped her up in the bed. "Those are stress induced, which is why you don't need visitors or to be talking to anyone right now. You need to rest."

"I know, but this is really important." Jessica let out a long sigh and relaxed.

"Nothing is more important than that little baby in your body right now. Whatever it is, it can wait. It's not life or death."

"But it is."

The nurse rolled her eyes. "What? Your husband didn't bring you the right shade of mascara for your hospital visit? You are having second thoughts about the color you painted the nursery? Relax. It'll be all right."

Jessica clenched her fists and seethed. Based on how she felt, she wanted nothing more than to plant a punch between the nurse's eyes. She thought better of it, relaxed her hands and nodded. "You're right. It'll be all right." She closed her eyes and waited.

The moment she heard the door latch, she opened her eyes to find the nurse gone. She grabbed her phone and dialed Cal's number.

"This is Cal Murphy."

"Cal, it's me—Jessica. I need your help."

"Now's not a good time."

She felt her heart rate rising, attesting to the increased pace of beeps on her monitor. "I really need your help. I'm here in Phoenix now, and things have spiraled out of control since we last spoke."

"Seriously—it's not a good time."

She ignored him. "I got a call from some random guys

threatening me if I didn't pay them a half-million dollar debt that they are saying Tanner racked up. I passed out in the parking lot at the track and woke up in the hospital, where Ned Davis visited me. He offered me what amounts to hush money if I drop the investigation and renounce the findings. I just don't know what to do." She began to cry.

"Look, Jessica. I'm sorry—I really am. I want to help, but I can't right now. In fact, I'm done. I've got my own problems I'm dealing with now, starting with the fact that I no longer have a job. But even worse, somebody has threatened my wife. And that's the end of that. I won't be pursuing this story any longer."

"But you have to. You can't just—"

"I can and I have, Jessica. I've got a wife and a daughter to worry about. And no story is so big that it trumps my family's safety. I'm really sorry, but I wish you the best of luck."

"Cal Murphy, I swear to God—" she said before the line went dead.

She threw her phone across the room and seethed, trying to ignore her increased heart rate. It was all she could think about.

The nurse stormed into the room and noticed the phone missing from the bedside table. "What did you do?"

"I think I'm having another contraction."

"What happened to get you so worked up? This isn't normal."

Jessica said nothing before she turned pale and fainted.

CHAPTER 36

KELLY MURPHY PRESSED the redial button again and muttered under her breath. It wasn't like Cal to ignore her calls and fail to call her back unless something was wrong. More often than she'd like to remember, things had gone wrong for Cal while investigating various stories. It wasn't a nightmare she wanted to relive again, but her stomach sank when her latest attempt to reach him ended in a direct-to-voicemail answer.

"Come on, Cal. Pick up your phone," she said aloud before tossing her phone onto the couch.

She paced around the living room and pondered what other way she might be able to reach him. Never one to assume the worst, she wondered if maybe her deep-seated fears were being realized once again.

As she paced around the room, she glanced out of the window. She'd noticed a car parked along the road in her neighborhood. She wasn't watching it that closely, but her intermittent glances was enough to tell her it had been there at least three hours without moving. While she couldn't be certain, she would've almost sworn the driver never got out. Now, she wanted to know why he was there.

Am I paranoid or what?

204 | JACK PATTERSON

She meandered to the kitchen and poured herself a glass of wine. She needed to think—and relax.

Earlier in the day, her mother came over and volunteered to take Maddie for the weekend. Not that Kelly really needed the alone time. She preferred to have something to keep her busy when Cal was traveling, and taking care of Maddie provided the best diversion possible. However, she'd managed to keep herself occupied with examining the pictures Cal sent her.

It didn't take her long to realize they were fakes. She would never admit to Cal that a tinge of doubt crept into her mind. Yet she almost dismissed the thought as it first came to her. *Cal? At a strip club?* She chuckled at the thought. *He'd probably have no idea what to do.*

She was tempted to call Folsom and give him a piece of her mind, but she thought better of it. *Let Cal fight his battles. You just need to give him the ammo.*

Five minutes sitting down was all she could take before she grabbed her phone and dialed his number again. And again—nothing.

She peered out the window and the car was still there, parked in the same place. Only this time, she saw a flash of something.

What was that?

She turned off the lights and walked up the stairs. If someone was watching, she didn't want to make them think she was onto them. She turned on the bedroom light and then the bathroom light, both visible from the side of the house. But then she crept into Maddie's room. Aside from a thin ray of light streaming into the room from the hallway, it was dark. Kelly poked her head above the windowsill, just high enough to glimpse the car. The streetlight illuminated the front license plate numbers, which she typed into her phone.

She slumped down against the wall and called a friend at the FBI. Cal had made plenty of FBI contacts during his investigations, and they proved invaluable during times like this.

"Hey, Harry. This is Kelly Murphy. How are ya?"

"Good, Kelly. To what do I owe the pleasure of this call tonight?"

"I've got a tag I want you to run for me."

He laughed. "Do I look like a website?"

"If I could Google it, I would."

"Well, all right. If it's for you, Kelly, I'll do it."

"Thanks."

She gave him the numbers and letters—and waited. In the meantime, she poked her head above the windowsill to check again. *Still there.*

"You still there?" he asked.

"Yep. What've you got?"

"That car is registered to a Collin Langdon Beaumont of Matthews, North Carolina."

"Great. Thanks, Harry."

"Anything else I can do for you? You're not in trouble, are you?"

"Not right now, but that might change. I'll call you if I need something else."

"You know where to find me."

Kelly ended the call. "Collin Beaumont?" A quick web search revealed that Collin Beaumont was J.T. Beaumont's cousin. Collin raced dirt tracks in North Carolina and all over the South. He was also passed over for a driver gig on one of the lower circuits in favor of J.T. But according to one article she read, J.T. and Collin remained close friends.

What is he doing outside my house?

Without allowing for any plausible explanation, Kelly went to the worst place possible: Collin Beaumont was there to harm her. She began to review the protocol Cal helped establish for her in the event of such an emergency. He created a panic room for her underneath the stairs, equipped with cameras displaying all the rooms in the house. They could even be activated in the dark using infrared mode. It was something Cal did as a safety measure, but Kelly suspected he did it just so they could check on Maddie while she was sleeping—or to see if she was sleeping at all.

She dialed Cal's number again.

"Come on, come on. Pick up your phone," she muttered.

Straight to voice mail.

She growled before burying her face in her hands.

"What is going on?"

Kelly spun around and peered through the window again at Collin's car. It was still there—but he wasn't.

She jumped up and raced downstairs toward the panic room at the bottom of the stairs. She typed in the code on the keypad and slipped inside. Firing up the monitors, she waited as the TVs came to life and displayed the images in and around the house. Nothing.

Where'd he go?

She called Cal again. "Will you please pick up your phone?"

Nothing.

She texted him. And waited.

Still nothing.

Kelly decided she needed to determine what was happening right outside her house first and put her phone down. She studied the monitors transmitting images of the perimeter of the house.

The man was nowhere to be found.

CHAPTER 37

CAL DROPPED HIS CAR off at the Phoenix airport rental site and boarded a shuttle bus for the airport. He kept his head down and cut his eyes in both directions. While he hadn't gathered definitive proof, he felt someone was watching him. And he had to lose whoever it was.

Cal decided to resist the urge to join the race to the check-in stand, hoping to shorten the list of potential assailants following him. Instead of a busload, he narrowed it to three men, as everyone else thundered ahead of him to secure their tickets.

One of the men peeled off toward the restroom, leaving Cal to determine which of the two men it was. He spotted a trashcan that provided a clear enough reflection. He made his way toward it before stopping a few feet short of it. Cal dug out his ticket from his bag and glanced at the reflection. One of the men kept moving, while the other stopped and made a phone call on his cell phone over a hundred feet behind him. Cal glanced over his shoulder to see the man pacing about as he chatted on the phone. It was either a phone call to report on Cal's whereabouts or a ruse to avoid being noticed. Either way, it didn't work.

Cal seared the image of the man into his memory—

about six-foot-one, two hundred pounds, goatee, black sweatshirt, red baseball cap, jeans.

Time to fly.

He procured his boarding pass and headed toward the terminal. Upon entering the security line, Cal turned around to see if the man was still following him. He chuckled to himself as he noticed the man had purchased a newspaper and was peering above it in Cal's direction.

I hope this works.

Cal followed security protocol and was standing on the other side of the checkpoint in a matter of seconds without incident. Another quick glance. The man was still there.

Cal checked his watch. Forty minutes until the flight was scheduled to take off. He hustled toward the gate and almost immediately his zone was called to board.

Once he showed his ticket to the gate attendant, he lumbered down the jetway until it stalled out a few feet from the door.

"Happens every time," a passenger in front of him grumbled.

"Excuse me?" Cal said.

"Oh, these lines. Nobody ever pays much attention to the announcements on how to help expedite the boarding process. It's ridiculous."

Cal nodded and smiled. "Are you a Panthers' fan?" he asked, pointing to the man's hat.

"You know it. You headin' home, too?"

"Can't stay away from the Queen City for too long," Cal answered.

Moments later, the line resumed moving as the passengers plodded toward their seats.

Cal stole a look at the man's boarding pass. He was seated in a center seat on a row of three, while Cal had the aisle seat on the emergency row.

The line stalled again and Cal's new friend turned over his shoulder and said, "Another genius trying to cram his carry-on in the wrong way. How difficult is it for people to understand what 'wheels first' means? Geez."

Cal bobbed his head. "First they make us cram our stuff in here, then they shoehorn us in. Crazy. Where have they got you today?"

"Middle seat," the man said before groaning.

"Well, how about I make your day?"

"Oh?"

Cal grabbed his shoulder. "I recently injured my arm while golfing and know that I'd be absolutely worthless in the event of a water landing where I'd have to open the door for everyone. I'm in the emergency row. Wanna trade?"

The man turned all the way around. "You're serious?"

"As a heart attack."

"Well, if you're offering, I'm totally down for it. I've been dreading this flight all week for that very reason."

"I don't mind—and I'd feel terribly guilty if I couldn't get the door open for anyone."

"Sounds good to me."

Cal offered his boarding pass to the man, who gave him a quizzical look. "Just in case the flight attendants question us."

They swapped boarding passes and continued to their new seats.

Cal's original seat was farther back than his new one, but he doubted the guy minded since Charlotte was his final destination—and they had a four-hour flight ahead of them.

For the next fifteen minutes, passengers finished filing on the plane until it was full. One of the flight attendants made the announcement that the doors were about to close.

It's now or never.

Cal pressed his call button and swung into action—short breaths and flailing hands, followed up with a dramatic outburst.

"I'm gonna die. We're all gonna die. I need to get off this plane," he shouted.

Two flight attendants rushed toward him. "Sir, are you all right?"

"Do I look all right? I'm going to die if I stay on this plane."

"Sir, I can assure you that these planes are safe."

"I can't do it. I can't do it. Get me off of here right now!"

"Grab your stuff and follow me," one of the flight attendants said.

Cal grabbed his carry-on suitcase and computer bag and followed her. He continued the charade until he was standing outside the gate.

"Sorry, ma'am. I have a fear of flying. My doctors said I was cured, but I never believed them. Sorry to cause so much trouble."

The woman shook her head and touched his arm. "It's okay, honey. You keep seeing that therapist. You'll make it back on one day without incident."

Cal nodded and mouthed "thank you" again to the woman before heading toward the exit.

***

THE MAN ADJUSTED his red cap and stared at the woman behind the counter. "I was wondering if you might be able to help me," he said. "I've got a friend who was supposed to be on a flight headed for Charlotte. Can you tell me if he got on the plane?"

"I'm sorry, sir, but I can't divulge that kind of information due to privacy laws."

He slammed his hands on the counter. "I've got a brother who has a severe phobia of flying and I wanted to see if he actually made it on a flight tonight."

The agent sighed. "Which one?"

"Flight 362 to Charlotte."

"Just a second." She typed furiously on the keyboard before her screen revealed something. "What's the name?"

"Cal Murphy."

"Let me see." She banged away on the keyboard until she scribbled down a few notes. "It's a full flight and every seat is taken."

"And he's on there?"

The man glanced over his shoulder. He thought he'd noticed Cal walking past. He did a double take and he was gone.

"Yep."

He started to leave before she blurted out something else.

"No, wait. Oh, yes. He's on there. Someone else got off the flight with a panic attack, but it wasn't him."

She hadn't finished her sentence before he darted down the concourse in the direction he thought he'd seen Cal walking. He wove in and out of passengers in search of Cal. He ran outside toward the shuttle bus bay and scanned the line of passengers.

Nothing.

He sprinted toward the front of the line and watched one of the buses begin to roll. Running down the side, he strained to see inside the tinted windows.

Then he noticed Cal.

CHAPTER 38

OWEN BURNS FINISHED HIS DINNER and returned
to the hotel, with little conversation. It wasn't unusual for
him to go quiet on the night before a race. He always had
plenty on his plate and his crew gave him all the space he
needed to process and ponder what needed to take place in
order to achieve the best finish on the track. But Burns' mind
was anywhere but on the track tonight.

He washed up in his room before he decided to meander
downstairs for a drink.

Burns sat down at the bar and ordered a gin and tonic.
Slumped over his glass, he stared at the liquid and wondered
how he'd ended up here, in this place, in this moment, in
this stage of his life. He'd made friendships that would en-
dure long after he left the sport. And one of those friends
was gone, likely at the hands of someone else he believed to
be his friend. It made him sick to think about.

"You look like you could use some company," a woman
said as she slipped onto the seat next to him.

Burns didn't look up. "I could use another drink."

"Rough night?"

Burns recognized the fishing expedition the woman was
on. He refused to bite.

"Rough week."

"Wanna talk about it?"

Burns grunted and signaled for the bar tender to get him another drink.

"If it's all the same to you, lady, I prefer to be left alone. Got a lot on my mind."

She put her hands in surrender and slipped down the bar next to another unaccompanied man staring at his drink.

"Desperation is so unattractive," a woman whispered into his ear.

He turned around and saw Alexa Jennings.

"Who peed in your cornflakes?"

He took another sip and set his glass down. "Todd Cashman. The jerk won't let me check out the video footage from his truck."

"And you thought he'd just hand it over?"

"I held out hope that there was a sliver of humanity left in the man."

She scooted out the bar stool next to him and sat down. "You put far too much stock in your fellow humans. Don't you know everyone is prone to let you down—especially Cashman."

Burns shook his head. "My plea to help us quickly turned into how the revelation of such news would ruin his image and detract from his victory. He declined—and not so gracefully either."

"So, what are you gonna do now? Do you still need my help?"

"We're gonna get that tape—and you're gonna help me do it right now."

She stood up. "I'll get my coat."

Burns waved her off. "You won't need your coat."

CHAPTER 39

CAL FISHED HIS CAP out of his bag and pulled it down low on his face. He donned his jacket and pulled the collar up. The less recognizable, the better. By his best calculations, he only needed to disguise his face for another ten minutes before he could get his own transportation again.

He slumped into his seat on the open-air shuttle and scanned his fellow passengers' faces. With the images of his attackers seared into his memory, he'd know it if he saw them.

Seated in the middle of the shuttle, he glanced left. A pair of couples relived their exciting week in Phoenix and discussed how much money they won at the blackjack tables—and they wanted to share these memories with everyone else on the bus.

Cal glanced right. A loner in tattered jeans hugged his guitar case. Two men dressed in suits typed furiously on their smart phones.

Cal relaxed and began to wonder how sophisticated the people tailing him were. Did they bug his phone? Did they put a GPS tracker on him? He couldn't be sure, but he doubted it. If they were more high tech than he surmised, he hoped incompetence or laziness would supersede their capacity to find him.

His phone buzzed. It was Kelly.

He wanted to answer it and tell her that he was okay—for now. But he didn't want to reveal to anyone that he was on the lam, even if he felt like he'd correctly profiled the shuttle's passengers.

Cal touched the screen and sent the call straight to voice-mail.

She'll forgive me later.

The bus made a hard right and lurched upward toward the drop-off point outside the car rental terminal. Once the bus stopped, Cal waited as passengers boxed him in while reaching for their luggage. He exited the bus and headed for one of the terminals downstairs.

Cal's palms began to sweat as he walked downstairs. If Cal had a rap sheet, it would've looked harmless enough. Breaking and entering in college for a prank on a classmate, dash and dine on a dare, failure to pay a parking ticket. And though none of them earned him any jail time or even a note on his record since he'd never been caught, he considered what he was about to do—and what would happen if he did indeed get caught this time.

His cadence down the steps felt ominous to him. Something bad was about to happen—he just hoped it wasn't going to happen to him. But at this point, he felt as if there was no other choice.

In the bowels of the car rental garage, Cal identified one of the understaffed, discounted outfits. He recognized it as a startup company hoping to wedge its way into an already saturated market. By the looks of it, he figured they wouldn't be around much longer. The cars were already five deep and there was only one person processing harried customers, who were itching to get to the airport for their departure flights.

Perfect.

Cal snuck closer and laid his luggage around a corner, out of sight. He pulled out his cell phone and began tapping on it as he approached the woman at the end of the line. She huffed and stamped her foot as she looked around for someone to help her.

"Turning your car in, ma'am?" Cal asked coolly.

She sighed. "Finally. Yes, I'm ready to go."

"Are the keys in the ignition?"

She cut her eyes toward him. "This isn't the first time I've rented a car, bucko."

"Why don't I just email you your receipt and you can be on your way?"

"Fine. Can you help me with my bags?"

Cal forced a smile and hoisted the woman's overweight luggage onto the ground. He pulled up the handle for her. She jammed a rolled-up dollar bill into his hand.

"Thank you," he said. He pretended to check the odometer and tap on his cell phone until she disappeared into the elevator.

A whole dollar?

Cal jumped into the car and started to drive. He didn't get more than ten feet before the customer who had been in front of the woman banged on his window. "What about me? I was here first," the man said as he threw his hands up.

Cal swerved around him and turned the corner. He put the car in park and darted out to get his belongings. Then he was back in the car, heading toward the exit.

It was the perfect crime since no one would know the

car had been stolen—at least, not until a certain woman called about a missing receipt. But by then, it'd be safely back in the rental car company's possession with a head-scratcher of a riddle to solve.

Cal gunned it through a large swath of empty spaces. He whipped around a corner and was forced to hit the brakes.

The man who'd been following him to the airport stood in front of his car with his gun trained on Cal.

CHAPTER 40

INSIDE THE SAFE ROOM, Kelly pressed her feet against the door and leaned hard into the wall behind her. She called Cal again for the tenth time—or maybe the twelfth. By this point, she'd lost count.

Come on, come on. Pick up the phone!

Straight to voicemail—again.

This is getting old, Cal.

She ended the call and rubbed her face with both hands. With a deep breath, she tried to regain her composure. It wasn't an easy task given that someone was staked out just down the street watching her—and that he was now missing from his car. The fact that Cal had lost his job over some ridiculous accusations didn't help either. She wanted to punch somebody.

Kelly looked at the monitors again. No signs of any motion around the house.

While she waited for Cal to call her back, she decided to break the news to Folsom that someone had duped him.

"Folsom."

"This is Kelly Murphy."

"Oh, hey, Kelly. How are you?"

"I'd be doing much better if you weren't firing my

husband for things he didn't do."

"Now, wait a minute. I told Cal we'd look into it but I didn't have a choice as I got an ultimatum from upstairs."

"You are still ignoring the facts."

"I just passed along all the facts I had, which was Cal was in a strip club on a company trip running up a huge tab on the company credit card."

Kelly banged her fist on the wall. "You didn't even give Cal the common courtesy to ask him if he did it before you fired him."

"I promised him I'd look into it after he got back."

"You need to reinstate him now and issue an apology—or I'm coming after you with a wrongful termination lawsuit."

"Come on. Don't be absurd. I still don't have any proof contrary to what was sent to me."

"I do. Cal sent me those pictures and I analyzed them. Any idiot who's worked in a photo department and used Photoshop more than five minutes could recognize that these were faked."

"That's not what one of our photo journalists said."

"Was it an intern?"

"If you can prove it to me, Kelly, come on down here. We'll be putting the paper to bed shortly and you can show me what you're talking about."

"I can't exactly do that right now."

"And why's that?"

"Someone is watching me right now and making sure I don't leave the house."

"How convenient."

"I'm not lying, Folsom. It's somebody connected to the

story Cal's chasing right now."

"Yes, the story I warned him not to pursue. And now you're in danger. He should've listened to me."

"Maybe if you tried to support him instead of falling for some stupid picture someone sent you in an email, maybe he wouldn't be in danger—or me either."

"Spare me, Kelly. I think Cal's a helluva reporter, but I'm not gonna stick my neck out for him when he's acting like a crazy person. I told him this could happen, but he didn't want to hear it."

Kelly then dropped the phone and pressed her face close to the floor.

"Kelly? Kelly? What's going on?"

She collected the phone and inched it toward her face. "Someone just fired a shot into the house—and I don't know where it came from."

"I'll call the police."

"No! That'll only make it worse. I'll take care of this and call you back once it's sorted out."

She hung up and lay prone, motionless.

Cal had paid good money to train her for a moment like this. She hoped she could recall everything quickly. Her life depended on it.

CHAPTER 41

JESSICA TANNER ITCHED her arm where the port injected fluids into her body. She was now awake, maybe more so than at any other point in her life. Powerful forces swirled at work around her. Some she recognized, others she didn't. But it was all the same to her: Somebody wanted to suppress the truth about Carson's death.

She tried calling Cal again in hopes that he might reconsider and help her. It seemed so unlike him to not help after making a special effort earlier. Something seemed off.

No answer.

What is going on?

Lying in bed, she stared at the ceiling and wondered how her life had taken such a drastic turn in less than a week. Last weekend she was cozied up with Carson in a hotel room watching a movie and talking about the future. This weekend, she was a widow, alone in a hospital room, wondering if she had much of a future.

Her phone buzzed, alerting her to a call from one of her friends.

"Hey, Jessica. How are you?"

"Hi, Cassidy. I'm somewhere between lousy and worse. I'd be better off if I weren't in a hospital bed right now."

"Oh, no. Which hospital? I'll come get you."

"You'll have a long ride ahead of you—Phoenix General."

The woman laughed. "I'm actually in Phoenix, too. Bill surprised me with a weekend getaway. We flew out here and rented an RV and I'm sitting in RV city right now."

"Well, come on down. I'm in Room 425. I think it's after visiting hours, so tell them you're my sister or something so you can come up here."

"Will do. See ya in a bit."

Jessica put her phone down and glanced at the door as it swung open.

A new doctor staring at a chart in his hand strode toward her bed.

"Mrs. Murphy? I'm Doctor Banner."

She scooted up in the bed. "Hi, Doc. How are things looking?"

He sighed and shrugged his shoulders. "So far, so good. But I want to look a little closer at some things."

Dr. Banner put the clipboard down and pulled out his stethoscope. He listened for Jessica's heartbeat.

"Sounds good," he said. "Deep breath for me."

She took several deep breaths as he moved his stethoscope around her back.

He stepped back and scowled. "I'm not liking the sound of that."

Jessica sat upright. "The sound of what?"

"I think there might be an issue with your lungs."

"What kind of issue?"

"I can't say for certain but we need to run some more tests."

"Is that safe with me being pregnant?"

"Mrs. Tanner, this is no joke."

Jessica froze. She'd heard that line before and it sounded eerily familiar.

"Excuse me?"

"I said this is no joke. Lung issues aren't anything to play around with."

"Where's the consent form?"

Dr. Banner flipped through the chart. "It's not here, apparently. Let me go get one and I'll be right back with it so we can get started on your tests."

The moment the door closed behind him, Jessica ripped the port out of her arm and detached several other nodes stuck to her body. The monitor started beeping and she yanked the plug out of the socket. She scrambled to get dressed and stuffed everything else into her bag.

She crept toward the door and opened it, peering down the hall in both directions. She noticed Dr. Banner at a central counter, talking to a nurse and passing papers back and forth.

She waited until his back was turned and dashed out the door and toward a stairwell.

Once she traveled down several flights, she stopped to catch her breath. She called Cassidy.

"Where are you?" Jessica asked.

"About ten minutes away. Why?"

"Don't come in. I'll meet you in the parking lot."

"Is something the matter?"

"I'll tell you all about it when you get here."

"You're scaring me, Jessica. Are you going to be okay?"

"I'll be fine once I'm with you. But please hurry. I think someone here is trying to kill me."

CHAPTER 42

OWEN BURNS AND ALEXA flashed their access credentials at the gate to the garage and pleaded with the guard to let them in.

"It's after hours, you two," the guard said. "Sorry. No exceptions."

"Come on, man. I left my tickets to tonight's Lady Antebellum concert in the hauler. You've gotta let us go back in and get them."

The guard shook his head. "What part of 'no exceptions' do you not understand?"

Burns glared at him, but Alexa pushed him to the side as she infringed on the guard's personal space.

"What time do you get off work?" she said as she glanced as his naked ring finger. "We might have a backstage pass for you, too."

"I'm off in thirty minutes," he said.

She patted his face. "Sounds like a date to me."

He blushed. "Well, okay. Fine. But I need you two to be back here in fifteen minutes. I can't have you scampering out so close to the shift change or else I might lose my job."

"You got it, sugar," Alexa said as she followed Burns through the gate.

They walked for several yards before she said, "Is that all you needed me for?"

"That was the warm-up. The real challenge is next."

Burns looked over his shoulder at the guard, who waved at him. They headed toward their hauler and disappeared inside for a few moments.

"You ready to do this?" he asked.

"I've been doing this my whole life," Alexa said.

They exited the hauler through a door out of the guard's line of sight and crept around toward Todd Cashman's rig. Only the drivers of the haulers stayed in the trucks at night. It was a lonely job—just what Burns was counting on to help him get inside.

Alexa rapped on the driver's door at Cashman's hauler.

After a few seconds, a scruffy face peered through the privacy curtains drawn around the interior windows of the truck.

"What do you want?" the man yelled through the glass.

Alexa raised her eyebrows and winked. Burns crouched around the front of the truck, out of sight.

The driver held up a finger and disappeared behind the curtain. When he returned, he was wearing a cap and a nicer shirt. The door flung open and he stumbled down the steps.

"Can I help you, Miss?"

Alexa wagged her finger at him and shook her head. "No need to call me, Miss. That would mean I'm polite and mind my manners."

A toothy grin spread across the man's face. "Well, what should I call you then?"

She edged closer and then threw her arms around his neck. "Why don't you call me Hurricane?"

"Hurricane? Why that?"

"I'm about to blow you away." She then kissed him, catching him off guard. However, he didn't fight it and didn't take long to return the full embrace.

Alexa didn't stop until she'd managed to wrangle his keys off his belt and hand them to Burns, who stole next to her and slipped off to get the object.

Burns rolled under the truck to the other side and unlocked the side door. He flipped on a few lights and searched for the security video system.

Most of the haulers contained a similar layout, and there weren't many places to hide such equipment. It didn't take long for him to locate it and then find the library of tapes in a cabinet under it.

He scanned for the date from the previous weekend and fingered it before stashing it into his coat. In an effort not to arouse suspicion, he slid the tapes together to eliminate a gap between the chronologically ordered arrangement. He turned the lights off, rolled back beneath the truck and delivered the keys into Alexa's waiting hand.

Alexa reattached the keys and then pulled back from the man.

"Wow!" she said. "If I didn't have a date with Jason Aldean tonight—" She shook her head and stepped back.

Burns peeked around the corner and noticed the smile on the man's face now appeared permanent.

She waved at the driver and walked backward until she disappeared around the front of the truck to join Burns.

"Let's go," he whispered.

They snuck back across the garage to the Davis Motor Sports team hauler. Burns fired up their security monitor and pushed the tape in. He started scanning the footage.

"What exactly are we looking for?" Alexa asked.

Burns hustled over to the fridge and pulled out a beer. "The snake."

"You plan on being here for a while?"

He nodded.

"Then bring me one too."

Burns returned with a beer for Alexa and they both started draining their drinks as they watched the footage.

"Wait, wait, wait. Go back," she said.

He reversed the footage.

"Whoa! Right there. Do you see that?"

"Yep."

Burns let the tape keep running. Several minutes later, the same person reemerged on the screen and looked around before he slid beneath Carson Tanner's car. When he slid back out, his face was clear for just a second, but it was enough for Burns and Alexa to identify him.

"Why that low-life scum bag," Burns muttered. "I'm gonna make him pay."

CHAPTER 43

CAL DIDN'T BLINK as he stared at the man standing in front of his car. With his gun trained on Cal, the man didn't move as he talked on his cell phone.

Cal assessed his predicament—and it didn't appear favorable. Someone was watching Kelly. He had defied the instructions given to him by a nefarious group and all that was left to do was kill him. At least, that's how he read the situation.

It's now or never.

Cal waited for the most promising moment, one in which the gunman glanced away. All he needed was a glance. Cal revved the engine and glared at the man lit up by the car's high beams.

Then the glance.

Cal stomped on the gas and ducked as his car roared toward the man. Before the assailant could escape the brunt of the car's path, Cal hit him with the car and sent him sprawling to the cement. Cal glanced in his side mirror and continued driving. He watched the man scramble to his feet and fire two gunshots in his direction. Neither one of the shots hit the car.

The tires screeched as Cal jerked the car left toward the exit. Horns honking and people shouting created an eerie dissonance in the bowels of the parking garage. Cal kept his foot on the accelerator and tightened his grip on the steering wheel.

He roared out of the garage and toward the exit for the I-10.

Cal checked his mirror for signs of any cars following him. So far, nothing. But he distrusted his mirror and turned around several times over the course of the next minute to assuage his fears. Still nothing.

Another minute passed and then red and blue lights flickered in his rearview mirror. Sirens wailed. Cal saw a pair of headlights lurch forward a quarter of a mile behind him as the patrol car swerved from behind a car in the slow lane.

Cal noticed a pharmacy on the corner ahead off to the right. He turned at the cross street and then whipped into the pharmacy parking lot. With his hat pulled down low on his face, Cal slumped in his seat. And waited.

He wanted more than anything to go straight to the authorities and tell them what was going on. But there'd be too many questions, not to mention a likely detainment of some sort. At that point, he'd become part of the story as opposed to the one telling it. And he was never going to let *that* happen if he could help it.

The seconds dripped past until the sirens came and went.

Guess they were after someone else.

He dashed inside because he needed a new phone. Despite his best efforts to get ahead, the people following him always knew what his next step was going to be. Cal assumed that meant he was far too predictable or they had tapped his phone. He wanted to believe it was the latter.

Inside the store, he combed the aisles for a pay-as-you-go cell phone. Cal didn't carry much cash on him, but he had enough to purchase the phone.

Back in the car, he dialed Kelly's number.

"Answer the phone, Kelly," he grumbled.

The call went to voicemail.

She probably doesn't recognize this number.

He left her a message: "Kelly, I wanted to let you know that you're being watched. Be careful. Use the safe room. Call me back when you get a chance."

As he pulled back onto the road and veered onto the I-10 exit, Cal called Jessica.

"Hello?" she answered.

"Jessica, it's me, Cal."

"I almost didn't pick up since I didn't recognize this number."

"Look, about earlier. I'm sorry I had to act like that, but I thought someone might be listening. I had to sell them on the fact that I wasn't going to help you."

"Thank God."

"Yeah, so, where are you?"

"I'm almost at the track. One of my friends was kind enough to come rescue me from the hospital. I think someone there was trying to kill me."

"Why would someone do that?"

She sighed. "You tell me. I can't keep track of all the reasons why, but I know they were. I left in a hurry."

"Okay, text me your location on a Google map when you get there and I'll come find you. We have a lot to discuss, but we don't have a lot of time."

He hung up and continued to stare into his rearview

mirror. No suspicious movements.

Twenty minutes later, he drove over a rise and the track lights served as a beacon for his final destination.

He checked his rearview mirror again.

What the—

Behind him, police car lights flashed in his mirror. He watched as the car swerved past one car and whipped into the lane behind.

This time there was no mistake about it.

They were after him.

CHAPTER 44

HUNCHED OVER NEAR THE FLOOR, Kelly dried her hands off on her pants. She picked up her weapon of choice and waited.

If she was going to escape this situation, she'd have to wait until the best possible moment to unleash her fury and land a knockout blow. Although she didn't like to think about it, she'd gone over this situation in her mind hundreds of times before. She hoped it would never happen again, despite the fact that it'd occurred more than once in the past. But here she was, this time prepared for whatever the attacker creeping around her house tried to subdue her with.

The cast iron skillet in her hand seemed to be a better choice given the circumstances. Cal had also put a bat and a handgun in her arsenal. She didn't want the bat used against her—and she didn't want to kill anyone, even if her life was in danger. A knockout blow would suffice.

She watched the monitors, refusing to blink. The man groped his way through the house, knocking over one of her favorite ceramic knickknacks she'd bought while in Costa Rica on vacation the year before. A little green frog with the words "Pura Vida" painted on its lily pad.

Why that little punk!

She clutched the skillet handle tighter and tried to breathe normally.

You can do this, Kelly.

He continued to move toward the foot of the stairs, right into her wheelhouse. She slipped on her night vision goggles, turned off all the equipment and crept out.

On all fours, Kelly looked up to see the man a few feet away, still unaware that she was in the room with him. With both hands clasped around the butt of his revolver, he moved quietly toward her.

Without a sound, Kelly rose up on her knees and whacked his kneecap. He staggered to the ground and suffered another blow to the face before he had time to react defensively or otherwise. He slumped to the ground.

The gun had fallen from his hand, and Kelly kicked it aside. He groaned before she delivered another smashing blow to his face.

"That's for shooting at me," she said.

She drew back the skillet again and walloped his face with the side of it.

"And that's for breaking my frog."

She crawled back into the safe room and pulled out a parcel of rope and duct tape. She tied him up before taping his mouth shut.

When she opened her front door, Phil Pearson, her nosy next-door neighbor, stood on the sidewalk dressed in a robe with his mouth agape.

"Are you all right, Mrs. Murphy?" he asked.

"Never better." She smiled.

"Oh, well, I thought I heard a ruckus going on at your house and something like a gun shot fired."

"Yeah, that'd be from the punk who tried to shoot me. But he's tied up right now."

He stared at her and said nothing.

"Since you're here, it'd be great if you called the cops for me and had this scumbag dragged away." She started walking toward her car and unlocked it with her fob.

"Where are you going?"

"I've gotta be somewhere. But take care of this for me, will ya? I'll be back shortly to explain everything."

She padded her left pocket to make sure she still had the thumb drive with all the images proving Cal's innocence. After a head nod to Phil Pearson, she climbed into her car and headed toward The Observer offices.

She dialed Folsom's number.

"I'm on my way," she said after he answered.

"So soon? What happened?"

"It's a long story, but just be ready. I'm not in a mood for any games from you." She paused. "Oh, and make sure your publisher is there, too. He needs to see this."

CHAPTER 45

CAL PULLED INTO THE Phoenix International Raceway parking lot between the track and RV city and skidded to a stop. He slung his bag over his shoulder, jumped out of the car, and took off running toward a throng of people gathered for the Lady Antebellum concert. He glanced over his shoulder to see two officers pursuing him on foot. With about a 50-yard lead, Cal figured that's all he would need once he pressed his way into the mass of people.

He darted into one section that allowed for a makeshift aisle before he headed straight into the crowd. Several people expressed their displeasure at his interruption with an obscene gesture or two. The people who bothered to yell at him couldn't be heard above the crooning of the country trio.

Cal wove between drunken revelers, teenage make-out sessions, and screaming fans.

Gotta love live concerts.

He kept his head down and sought for a discreet exit. Just as he spotted a way out, he also came across a man who seemed to be enjoying everything about the concert.

"Nice hat," the man said.

Cal pulled his cap off his head and eyed the man's cowboy hat. "I'll trade ya."

The man nodded and swapped hats with Cal.

"Thanks," Cal said before he hustled toward an opening.

Once he broke out of the crowd, he didn't stop. He noticed several more officers had arrived and were canvassing a perimeter around the crowd. Before the net closed in, Cal slipped behind a privacy gate and circled back toward the entrance.

Cal called Jessica.

"Where are you?" she asked.

"I'm almost there. I ran into a little trouble."

"Are you okay?"

"Don't worry about me. You relax and don't get stressed out. Your baby doesn't need all that."

"I don't need all this. And I'm hoping you can put my mind at ease real soon."

"Just sit tight. I'll be there in about five minutes."

He hung up and put his phone away.

Cal watched the cars continue to stream in and out of the parking lot. Occasional honks and screams rose above the constant melodies rising from the concert stage a few hundred yards away. Then Cal turned his attention toward RV city, where smoke swirled upward intermittently from the small fires warming fans who remained outside in the cool desert air.

He looked at his screen and started to walk toward the GPS location Jessica had texted him.

Glancing up infrequently to make sure he didn't wander into the path of a vehicle or a bike taxi, Cal was staring down when he felt a firm hand slam into his chest.

Cal looked up. It was a Maricopa County Sheriff's deputy.

"Where do you think you're going?" the deputy asked.

Cal scanned the area, unsure if he'd actually been caught.

"Sir, I was just going to meet some friends in RV city."

"What's your name?"

Cal bit his lip. "Jim Waltrip."

"Jim Waltrip? THE Jim Waltrip?" The deputy gaped at him in disbelief.

While the Waltrip name might be royalty, Cal had no idea that there was a well-known Jim. Or maybe there wasn't and it just sounded famous to the deputy. Either way, it didn't matter as long as he let him go and didn't ask to look at his license.

"I gotta see this for myself," the deputy said as he chuckled. "Can I see your license?"

Cal put his hands all over his body and patted himself down before morphing his face into a scowl.

"I must've left it in the hauler," Cal said.

The deputy eyed him closely. "Is that so?"

"I can go fetch it for you, if you like."

The deputy didn't move and appeared deep in thought for a moment. "Look, just sign this for me and we'll call it good."

Cal scratched his first autograph onto the back of the deputy's citation pad and handed it back to him.

The deputy stepped aside and gestured forward with his left hand. "Have a nice evening, Mr. Waltrip."

Cal tipped his hat and kept walking. He wanted to look back, still in disbelief that he got away with it.

He was still within earshot when he heard one of the other deputies exclaim, "Jim Waltrip? There's nobody famous named Jim Waltrip, you idiot."

Cal quickened his pace as he turned down one of the alleys leading into RV city.

"Hey, wait! Come back here!" the deputy called.

Cal didn't heed his request, tossing his hat aside instead and weaving his way through RV city and toward Jessica.

CHAPTER 46

NED DAVIS HUFFED as he climbed the steps of the Davis Motorsports Team hauler. He opened the door and cracked his knuckles while he scanned the truck.

He stomped up the stairs and ripped open the door to the meeting room to find Alexa and Owen Burns sitting at the room's lone table.

Alexa looked up at him and smiled. "Is everything all right, honey?"

Davis slammed his fist on the table. "What the hell is goin' on here?"

She stood up and never took her gaze off his eyes. "What do you mean?"

"I just got a text from the security guard—the guy I pay extra on the side to keep an eye on what happens around here." Davis pulled out his phone and swiped a few times before hoisting it to eye level. "And this is what he sent me."

Alexa stared at the screen, a snapshot of her kissing the driver for the Cashman hauler. "It's not what you think."

"Oh, it's not, is it? And what's this?" He gestured toward Burns. "Are you trying to score with everyone tonight?"

Burns put his hands up. "It's not like that, Ned. I needed her help."

"Her help to do what? Piss me off?"

Burns stood up and put his hand on Davis' shoulder. "Just calm down and let us explain. It's not like that."

"Of course, it's not like that. It's never like that when you get caught. I can smell a snake a mile away."

Burns shook his head. "No, you're reading this all wrong."

"The only thing that's wrong here is that you're still employed by me. But I can fix that right now. You're fired. Now, get outta here."

Burns sighed. "Oh, come on, Ned. That's not what's going on here, and you know it. I'd never do anything like that to you."

Davis chuckled and pointed at Alexa. "But she would." He turned his gaze toward her again. "You little tramp."

Burns stepped between Davis and Alexa. "Just calm down, Ned. Give us a chance to explain."

"I'm sorry. Were you talking to me? You're fired. Now get out of my sight."

Burns took off his cap and ran his fingers through his hair. "You're making a big mistake."

"The only mistake I ever made was trusting you. Now leave before I go get security."

Burns snatched the tape and a thumb drive off the table and headed for the door.

"Wait," Davis said. "What is that in your hand?"

Burns turned around slowly. "I'm sorry. Were you talkin' to me? Because you're not my boss anymore and I've gotta get outta here before you call security."

Davis snatched Burns' access badge from around his neck. "This isn't funny."

"I'm not laughing. But good luck tomorrow. You and your two-bit driver are gonna need it."

"Holmes will do a fine job."

"At finishing last," Burns muttered. He slammed the door as he left.

Davis turned and grabbed Alexa's arm. "How dare you disrespect me like that! You're an embarrassment."

Alexa jerked her arm back and rolled her eyes. "If there's anyone who is an embarrassment right now, it's you."

He sneered as he stared her up and down. "You're pathetic."

She sat down and shook her head. "And tomorrow, you'll be through. No one will ever race for you again—if you even have a team."

CHAPTER 47

KELLY CLENCHED HER PHONE and hit redial as she navigated the streets of downtown Charlotte. This wasn't how she expected her Saturday night to go. With Maddie at her mother's, Kelly had anticipated a time of relaxing on the couch with some nice wine and a romantic mystery. Instead, the evening had devolved into hiding from an intruder, smashing him in the head with a frying pan, and trying to prove her husband wasn't a spend-a-holic who spent his free time on the road in strip clubs.

So much for the quiet evening.

She swerved off I-277 and onto the College Street exit.

Come on, Cal. What is your problem? Answer your phone.

Even dialing Cal's apparent new number, she couldn't get him to pick up. Her frustration turned to fear as her tires screeched while pulling into *The Observer* parking lot.

She hopped out of her car and hustled toward the front door, tapping on the glass to get the security guard's attention.

"Can I help you, miss?" the guard asked after he unlocked the door.

"I need to speak to Marc Folsom, the sports editor," she said.

The guard held up his index finger. "Wait just one minute."

After what felt like five minutes to Kelly, the guard returned and opened the door. "He just finished for the night and told me to send you up."

The guard gave Kelly directions to the news department and how to find Folsom before relocking the front door.

She stepped onto the elevator and rubbed the thumb drive in her right hand. The idea of sitting on the couch and reading served to be a far more alluring idea, especially at the moment. But Cal needed her—right now. She tried to suppress any thoughts of what he might be doing or how challenging life might be after getting falsely accused of doing something, even if it wasn't the first time.

In fact, Cal's life seemed to be a repetitious pattern of bad to worse. Nothing ever ran smoothly for him. It didn't bother Kelly too much. She knew what she was getting into when she signed up to marry him: an exciting life of adventure and not much stability. At the time, she didn't consider how she might want stability later on, choosing to dwell on the tantalizing adventure that awaited them. Yet she had to admit that taking flash drives down to his office at 11 o'clock at night to save his job wasn't exactly what she had in mind.

Stay calm, Kelly. Just stay calm.

The moment the elevator doors opened, she noticed Folsom standing across the newsroom joking with a colleague. She glanced at her reflection in the stainless steel elevator wall before stepping out. Even through the gross distortion, she could tell her cheeks were red—fire red.

She stormed across the room, toward Folsom. He never saw her coming.

"I've got half a mind to slug you into next week," Kelly said.

The employee talking with Folsom glanced at Kelly and excused himself.

"Now, Kelly—" Folsom began.

"No, there's no Kelly anything. I can't believe you had the audacity to fall for some half-wit amateurish prank—and all right in the middle of the biggest story your paper's covered in the past decade."

Folsom took a few steps back. "Let's take this into my office."

Kelly slapped a file folder on top of a desk to the left of Folsom. "No, we're doing this right here. You fired him publicly and I'm gonna clear his name publicly."

He put his hands out in a gesture of surrender. "Okay, Kelly. Please, calm down. I'm on your side."

"I hardly believe that. I don't care what you say."

"Believe what you must, but I want to get Cal reinstated as much as you do."

She rolled her eyes. "I doubt that." She pointed at the file. "It's all there."

He opened the folder. "What exactly am I looking at?"

"Several things. First, there's an enlarged printout of the digital file you were sent. I circled the areas that indicate it's a fake."

Folsom looked at it closely and nodded.

"Then there's our personal credit card receipt that is time stamped at the exact same time these credit card purchases were supposedly made. Somebody had to steal his card or the card number."

He nodded. "What else?"

She picked up another sheet of paper and handed it to him. "These are our phone records, indicating that at the time Cal was supposedly gallivanting around Phoenix, he was on the phone with me. Cal's got guts, but even if he ever did think about going to a strip club—which he wouldn't—he'd never have the courage to call me from one."

Folsom rubbed his chin with his free hand. "You seem pretty adamant he wouldn't do this."

"Cal likes being married to me."

He chuckled and closed the folder. "I can't really argue with anything in here. Let me talk to my publisher in the morning about this and we'll see what we can do."

Kelly stamped her foot. "No. You'll do it now." She reached over and picked up a phone off the hook and shoved it into Folsom's hands.

She stepped off to the side and let Folsom call his publisher to deliver the news.

After several moments of what looked like Folsom pleading, he finally smiled and hung up.

"Good news, Kelly. The publisher has decided to temporarily reinstate Cal until we can undergo a full evaluation. And to be honest, I'll be surprised if anything more is ever said of this."

She put her hands on her hips. "Oh, something more better be said of it—like an apology to Cal in front of the entire newsroom. I can't believe this kind of ridiculousness goes on here. You'd skewer any financial entity you cover that fired a star employee without cause. Don't suddenly act like you can just sweep this under the rug."

"Okay, Kelly. I get it. You think Cal was set up by someone and wronged by us. We'll do our best to make it right."

She sighed. "You better. Cal would sweat blood to get you a breaking story first."

"I know. I'll let you deliver the good news to him. Hopefully, you can convey how much I appreciate him when you speak with him."

"I'd love to tell him right now—if only he'd pick up his phone."

Kelly spun and turned toward the elevator at the opposite end of the room.

Once she reached her car, she climbed inside and dialed Cal's number again. After the second ring, he answered.

"Where have you been?" she asked.

"Long story. I've been trying to get ahold of you. Are you okay?"

"Long story. But I'm alive. Let's just say your panic room and monitoring equipment proved rather handy tonight."

"Where's Maddie?"

"She's with my mom. No need to worry. It was weekend with grandma."

Cal sighed. "That's a relief."

"Yeah, so here's what you need to know. I think the culprit is J.T. Beaumont—or at least somehow connected to him."

"Beaumont? Really?"

"Yeah, it was his cousin Clint Beaumont who was stalking me."

"How'd you find all this out?"

"I called one of your FBI buddies and he told me who owned the car of the man who was parked outside our house."

"And you found out he was Beaumont's cousin after that?"

254 | JACK PATTERSON

"Well, I verified it was the same guy by checking the driver's license in his wallet after I knocked him out with a frying pan."

"You did what?"

"Like I said, long story. Anyway, I did a quick search on Clint Beaumont and came across an article talking about how he and Beaumont used to race on a local dirt track circuit—and it mentioned they were cousins."

"Good work, detective."

"Where are you?"

"I'm talking to Jessica Tanner right now. She was threatened by some thugs about some supposed gambling debt her husband had. I wish I had more time to tell you about it."

"I wanna hear all about it when you get home. But I actually called to give you some good news."

"Oh? What's that?"

"You're temporarily reinstated."

"Temporarily?"

"It's not all great news, but Folsom called the publisher and said they'd investigate when you got back, after seeing all the evidence I presented. Plus, those photos were fake."

"Thanks, honey. I appreciate you believing in me."

She didn't say anything.

Cal took a deep breath. "You do believe in me, don't you?"

She waited for a moment again. "Cal Murphy, if you ever go to a strip club—" She broke out into a laugh.

"That's not funny, Kelly."

"Of course, I believe in you, Cal. Now be safe and go find out why Beaumont would want to murder Carson Tanner — and silence you."

"I think the answer's pretty obvious."

"It's never obvious, Cal."

***

CAL HUNG UP and turned to Jessica, who sat hunched over on a couch. She chewed her fingernails and stared through the window at the party-like atmosphere just outside.

"Anything?" she said.

"Yeah, that was my wife. A couple of good things. One, I'm reinstated, so I actually have an outlet to report this story. And two, Beaumont's cousin was the one monitoring her at our house in North Carolina tonight. It seems at least that J.T. Beaumont was involved somehow."

"And the bad?"

"I'm sort of a fugitive after I borrowed a rental car without proper authorization while somebody was trying to kill me. We need to return that car tonight before I become the subject of a manhunt."

"Is that all?" She stood up. "Let's go to the authorities with this right now and tell them the truth."

"It's not that simple, Jessica. We've got two people we need to take down—the person who sabotaged Carson's car and the person who's trying to get money out of you."

"And you think we can deliver proof to the police?"

"We've gotta try. If we don't make sure both these guys go to jail, you'll never be safe."

CHAPTER 48

EARLY SUNDAY MORNING, Owen Burns adjusted his Davis Motor Sports cap and waved at the guard standing by the tram stop just outside Phoenix International Raceway. The guard had been stationed there every morning and recognized Burns and his gear; he didn't even take the time to ask for his credential. Burns slipped past him and walked underneath the tunnel leading to the track infield.

He said hello to several of his friends who'd been on the circuit for as long as he had. If it weren't race day, they would've struck up a conversation with him. But now wasn't the time for small talk—it was time to focus in on the task at hand: winning.

However, Burns had a different task in mind.

Since his sudden firing, he managed to make several copies of the video depicting the tampering, complete with a time stamp. He'd have no problem causing a stir once he convinced a few journalists to look at the video. His biggest challenge was staring him in the face.

"I'm sorry, sir, where's your pass?" said the guard positioned by the garage gate.

Burns tapped his chest with his hands and then patted his pockets. "Aww, man. I must've left it at the hotel."

"Better hustle back."

"Seriously?" Burns stared him down. "I've got a job to do and I don't have time to run back to the hotel."

"I'd sure hate to have an absent-minded crew member like you working on *my* car."

"Hey, buddy, better stop with the wise cracks. I'll get someone over here in a minute."

The guard folded his arms and stared at Burns. "Go ahead, tough guy. I've got all day." The guard waved a few more crew members through.

Burns turned to one of the men walking through the gate. "Cory, can you vouch for me? This guy thinks I'm try-ing to sneak in."

Cory turned and nodded. "He's legit."

The guard snarled. "I don't care who vouches for you or if you're the NASCAR president's son. No pass, no entry. Got it?"

Burns seethed as he turned and stared at Rattlesnake Hill already filling up with spectators. He considered a new ap-proach.

"Look, how do you think I even got in here? One of the guards recognized me from being here all week and didn't have a problem with it."

The guard stroked his chin. "And that's why he's out there and I'm here. They put the best guards on this gate. Now scram back to your hotel and get your pass or beat it. I don't care."

Forget this.

Burns shifted to the side and sprinted through the gate past the guard. He didn't get more than twenty feet before his legs buckled and he crashed to the ground under the weight of the guard.

The guard stood up and yanked Burns up to his feet. "Let's go, buddy."

"Get your hands off of me," Burns said. He pulled the tape out of his pocket. "I've got proof of who killed Carson Tanner."

"Save it, will ya?" the guard said as he refused to release a fistful of Burns' shirt.

"Ned Davis is covering this up. Carson Tanner was murdered!"

"Enough!" the guard said. He marched Burns out of the gate. The scene created enough of a distraction that Burns heard the rumor mill cranking up around him.

"Did you see that?"

"Is that Owen Burns?"

"What's going on?"

"Is he drunk?"

The guard radioed for assistance and requested that someone escort Burns off the premises.

Burns hung his head and boarded the tram under the watchful eye of the guard. Once they reached the outside, the guard shoved him off the tram and told him not to come back until he had proper credentials.

"This ain't no Mickey Mouse show," the guard growled at Burns.

***

JACKSON HOLMES WALKED into the Davis Motorsports Team trailer and began looking over the checklist. He'd always dreamed of an opportunity to serve as a crew chief, though he never anticipated it coming in a situation like this.

Ned Davis walked into the trailer with two cups of coffee in his hand. "Long night?"

Holmes nodded. "Just wanted to make sure I've got everything ready to go here." Davis handed him a coffee. "I really appreciate the opportunity, sir."

"Well, you've been a faithful member of this crew and the one with the least amount of baggage. I figured it couldn't hurt to give you a shot with these last two races this season and see how you handle everything."

"I'll do my best. I don't know if I can do any better than Burns."

Davis chuckled. "Let's hope so. He was always the problem."

"You think so?"

"Absolutely. And if you ask me, he's gone a little nutty lately."

"How so?"

"He's convinced that all those reports are true about someone on this team sabotaging the car last week. I know all of you guys—and he's the only one I'd ever suspect."

"Yeah, he's been acting a little strange this week. I even saw him screaming outside the garage this morning."

"Burns?"

"Yeah, he tried to sneak past a guard, who took him down. The whole time Burns was screaming something about having proof that that car was sabotaged. He was waving something in his hand."

"Thanks, Holmes. I'll take care of this. You just focus on the race."

Holmes stared at his checklist while he strained to hear Davis, who'd stepped a few feet away and was talking softly into his phone.

"Burns is still out there and causing trouble," Davis said. "He took a tape from here last night and is claiming he has proof that Tanner's car was sabotaged last week." A pause. "I need you to take care of it."

Holmes swallowed hard and tried to focus on his list.

CHAPTER 49

FLANKED BY JESSICA, Cal settled into a chair across from Deputy Livingston's desk. Cal straightened the stapler hanging cockeyed off the desk and moved the nameplate flush with the edge. He glanced around the office for the deputy but didn't see him.

Cal reached for the deputy's coffee mug and felt it. "It's pretty warm," he said to Jessica. "He's not going to leave this here for long."

A few moments later, Deputy Livingston emerged from a room down the hall and strode toward his desk.

Cal stood up, as did Jessica. They both offered their hands as they greeted him.

"Have a seat," Livingston said. Everyone sat down and the deputy began scanning a folder on his desk.

He closed the folder and folded his hands. "So, what brings you two down here today?"

"I told you we'd talk soon," Cal said.

"You did, but you didn't tell me what about. I'm hoping this has something to do with Ronald Parker."

"It does, but there are also some other things involved."

"Such as?"

"Such as last night's manhunt for me."

"Come again?"

Cal cleared his throat and sat up straight. "Last night, I borrowed a rental car—which I've already returned, I might note—when someone was trying to kill me."

Livingston's eyes narrowed. "Why didn't you go to the authorities?"

"Long story, but I didn't have time. The people after me were watching my wife and threatened to kill her if I talked to you about it."

"And now it's suddenly okay?"

"My wife handled things on her end—with a cast-iron skillet. But that's not the main reason why we're here."

Livingston pulled his handcuffs off his belt and placed them on his desk. "I heard about that chase last night. Why shouldn't I charge and book you right now since you've admitted to this?"

"Well, I think it'd be a waste of your time and resources since the car was never stolen, I returned it and paid for a day's rental plus gas—and I think you'd rather bust the Goldini gambling ring."

"Wait a minute. What does any of this have to do with the Goldini family?"

"Are you a NASCAR fan?"

Livingston shook his head.

"Me neither. But I am a conspiracy nut—and there are plenty of stories about the Goldini family and how they've made numerous attempts to infiltrate NASCAR."

"They always skate."

"Yeah, but I think you can take out some of their people today if you're interested—and solve the Ronald Parker murder in one fell swoop."

Livingston pulled out a folder from his desk and opened it. "Ronald Parker died of a snake bite—at least that's the initial assessment from the coroner."

"I doubt that's entirely true."

"What do you mean?"

Cal took a deep breath. "I think Parker was a gambler and owed a big debt to the Goldini family."

"And what makes you think that? It's not like they keep books out in the open."

Jessica leaned forward. "Because the same people who tried to get money out of me from a debt Carson apparently ran up before he died had to be the same people who came looking for Ron Parker the night he died."

"Perhaps." Livingston eyed them both closely. "How do you both know all of this?"

Cal cleared his throat. "It's a long story, but I've been doing some investigating of my own related to something else—and these loose threads seem to be forming a sinister tapestry."

"Interesting," Livington said. "I've got something I want to show you."

He disappeared for a few minutes and returned holding an evidence bag containing a cell phone.

"What's this?" Cal asked.

"Ron Parker's cell phone."

"And why am I looking at it?"

"We found one on him that had been destroyed with the sim card removed. But we found this one hidden in his car."

"What's on it?"

"I was hoping you could tell us."

Cal's mouth hung agape. He replayed it for Jessica, who started to cry.

"Can I get a copy of this?" Cal asked.

"Sure. Just message yourself one right now."

Cal pressed a few buttons. "Thanks."

"So what were you saying about loose sinister threads? Does this video figure into any of this?"

"It might. And this video might help me prove it. And if I'm right, you won't have to wait long to bust the Goldinis."

"And how exactly are we gonna do that?"

Cal smiled. "I thought you'd never ask."

CHAPTER 50

IT WAS ONLY 9 A.M. and Cal felt like he'd already worked a full day. But there was no time to waste. All the players were converging at the track—or at least, they would be once his plan was fully set into motion. He felt like he'd spent the past few days in a fog, but he knew it would clear in a few hours if they could pull this off.

Cal walked through the gate leading to the garage area and watched all the cars undergoing their final pre-race tune-ups. He spied Sylvia Yates talking on her cell phone just outside the Davis Motorsports Team hauler.

"Good morning, Sylvia," he said with a smile.

She shook her head. "I wish I could say it was good." She shook his hand.

"Why? What's going on?"

"Davis fired Burns last night and replaced him with Jackson Holmes."

"He did what?"

"You heard me. And nobody knows why at this point—but apparently everybody on press row already found out."

"How's that?"

"Burns was escorted off the property, ranting and raving like a madman. Something about how he had a video that proved Carson Tanner's car was sabotaged."

Cal bit his lip and decided against tipping his hand about what he knew. "That's too bad."

She glanced back at him. "Too bad? I thought you'd be all over him by now since you've been hawking that story."

"I've had other issues to deal with lately. Personal issues."

She nodded. "Fair enough. So, you ready to interview the rising star, J.T. Beaumont?"

"Absolutely."

She started walking toward the hauler. "Okay, just keep it brief. He's got a sponsorship event in twenty minutes and he can't be late."

"Got it."

He walked into the hauler and she introduced him to Beaumont before exiting.

Cal wasted no time with pleasantries—nor did he resemble anything pleasant.

He lunged at Beaumont and put hands around his neck. "I don't know who you think you are, but I swear to God you're gonna pay for what you did." He shoved Beaumont once more before backing up.

Beaumont glared at him. "I don't know who you think you are, but how dare you come at me like that. I have no idea what you're talking about."

"Oh, really? Why don't you give your cousin a call—you know, the one who was staked outside my house last night, the same one who fired a bullet into *my* house."

Beaumont rolled his eyes and waved off Cal. "You're crazy, man. Again, I have no idea what you're talking about."

Cal lunged at him again, this time kneeing Beaumont in

the crotch. "I've got little patience for this stunt you're trying to pull."

"Hit me again and the cops will have to drag me off you."

Cal leaned in and prepared to take a punch. "Great. I dare you. It'll just lend more credence to my story that I'm about to publish. The one about how you orchestrated the sabotaging of Carson Tanner's car just to get this opportunity—and now you're trying to keep me quiet."

"You really have lost it."

"You're gonna lose everything by the time I'm done with you."

"Look, man, I don't know what your problem is, but you're crazy, okay? It's time for you to leave because I've got a job to do and some real interviews—and I don't appreciate getting threatened."

Cal knew he'd crossed too many lines but needed to draw a reaction out of Beaumont before his opportunity was gone. Everything was hinging on this—or so he thought.

He pulled his phone out of his pocket and showed a picture to Beaumont. "Recognize this guy?" Cal asked. It was a photo Kelly had snapped and sent to him of Beaumont's cousin after she'd knocked him out.

Beaumont pulled back and his eyes widened as he looked at the photo. He said nothing.

"That's what I thought," Cal said. "That was what my wife did to him. Now he's in jail."

Finally, Beaumont broke. "Look, man, I was just trying to scare you. I didn't mean anything by it. I didn't mean for anyone to get hurt."

"Oh, really? The only people who really got hurt are

your people—and my back, which didn't enjoy the ride in the trunk."

"I just told them to rough you up a bit. I didn't know they were going to do all that."

Cal seethed as he plotted his next words. "You didn't know they were going to shoot at my wife? That is beyond ridiculous. I don't believe a word out of your mouth."

Beaumont stepped back. "Honest, man. I wasn't trying to hurt anyone."

Cal poked his finger into Beaumont's chest. "The only thing I want to know now is who you paid to sabotage Carson Tanner's car last week."

"Now, you've gone off the reservation. I had *nothing* to do with that. *Nothing.*"

"And why should I believe you now, since you've already spent the last five minutes lying to me?"

"Because it's the truth. Look, racing is a like a big fraternity. We don't always like each other, but nobody wants to see anyone end up dead, certainly not Carson Tanner. He was a good dude."

"So, why'd you threaten me like this?"

"I never meant to hurt you. But your story had the potential to blow up this team and I've waited a long time to get a shot to drive at this level. I didn't want you screwin' it up with some muckraking report."

Cal pulled his phone out of pocket, displaying a large red circle and a timer ticking upward. "Looks like you just did it for yourself."

Beaumont reached for Cal's phone. Cal pulled it back and grabbed a wrench lying next to a toolbox. "Don't make me turn you into a clone of your cousin."

"I'm gonna hunt you down. You better never let your guard down."

"I'll be ready. Don't you worry," Cal said.

Beaumont turned and exited the hauler.

Cal waited for a few moments before following him. Sylvia Yates' eyes were wide as her gaze met Cal's.

"What was that all about?" she asked.

"You don't wanna know. But I'll tell you this—and I say this with the greatest sympathy—I just made your life hell."

CHAPTER 51

JACKSON HOLMES GLANCED around the garage area at the hive of activity at the hauler. He looked back down at his checklist and continued to move through it methodically. A door slamming shut startled him and he shot a look toward the hauler again to see Beaumont storming off and Sylvia Yates following after him while trying to talk back over her shoulder to Cal Murphy.

"What's goin' on over there?" Dirt asked as the commotion gave him reason to pause from his detailed work.

"Beats me," Holmes said.

"It's like we've turned into a damned soap opera around here," Dirt said before returning to his duties.

"Ain't that the truth?"

Holmes bit his lip and appeared to look at the engine, while stealing glances beneath the cover of his cap at Beaumont storming away.

Russ Ross tugged on the safety harness inside the car. Once he pulled his head out, he caught Holmes staring in Beaumont's direction.

"He'll have his head in the race," Ross said. "Don't you worry."

"I'm not. Anything will beat Tanner's pre-game antics,

tryin' to hug the neck of every sick kid in a three-state area everywhere we went."

"That had nothin' to do with it," Ross said. "He just couldn't drive—period. Huggin' necks or not."

Holmes shook his head. "I hope that's all it was. And I hope Beaumont's ready. We may not win a championship, but I want us to end this season with a bang."

"Speakin' of explosions, here comes Alexa," Dirt said.

"I heard that," she said as she sauntered up to the car. She bent down and stuck her head over the engine, right next to Dirt's. She then made a clucking noise with her tongue as she pulled her head out from beneath the hood. "You might want to check this again," she said, gesturing toward the area where Dirt was working. "I don't trust this guy."

Dirt huffed and rolled his eyes. Holmes didn't move.

"He's been known to miss a few things here and there," she said.

Holmes waved dismissively. "I trust him. Why don't you let us handle the big boy stuff here and you go back to doing what you do best—whatever that is."

She shot him a look. "You mean, let you handle it like you did last week?"

"Knock it off, Alexa," Ross said. "We don't need this—not now or ever."

"Yes, Alexa, we have to work to do," Holmes said. "So, if you'll excuse us—"

She tossed her head back and flipped her hair over her shoulders. "Don't worry. I'll go for now. But I'll be back soon enough—sooner than you'd like, I promise."

CHAPTER 52

JESSICA TANNER FIDGETED with the wire running along the inside of her bra. She stopped and stared at the FBI agent holding his hands out to help her. She swatted him away.

"I got this," she said. "Can you give me some privacy here?" She situated the wire and smoothed out her shirt.

The agent backed away and sat across from her on a couch in the RV. "Are you sure you're up for this?"

She crossed her legs and took a deep breath. "Not really, but it's the only way I'm ever gonna get any peace."

"You do realize this might make you more of a target, if we aren't able to put these guys away?"

"Damned it I do, damned if I don't. Besides, if they come after me later, maybe I can pay off Carson's debt. In the short term, this is what's best. I need to put all the money I get in the hands of capable surgeons instead of thieving thugs."

"I guess you know what you're doing then. Do you want to go over this one more time?"

She checked her phone. It was 10:30 in the morning and she was already on her third cup of coffee. "I've got it down."

"Good luck."

She dialed the number back that the caller had used to make the initial threat.

"Hello. Who is this?"

"This is Jessica Tanner and you called me about a debt my husband owed you."

"Yeah?"

"Well, you told me I have a week to pay up, but I'd like to take care of it today."

"Today?"

"Yes, in two hours at the Phoenix International Raceway."

"Lady, last time I talked to you, you said you didn't have any cash. How do I know this isn't a set up?"

"Because I'm going to have enough money to pay off his debt, and I got a generous man to forward some of it to me."

"I read you weren't gettin' any money because of his crappy life insurance policy. That had to suck, huh?"

She took a deep breath. "Well, that's all about to change."

"Is it?"

"Yes, just keep watching the news. If you don't hear anything that makes you think otherwise before noon, don't come. Otherwise, I'll see you here at 12:30. I'm texting you the location right now."

For a moment, silence. Then, "Okay, I got it. I'll be watching. And if you're lying to me, I'm going to add a late payment fee."

"I'll be waiting." She hung up.

The FBI agent leaned forward and patted her on the

knee. "Excellent work. Do you think he bought it?"

"Sounded like it to me."

"Great. This could be huge for the agency to catch these guys like this."

"It'll be great as long as Cal Murphy comes through on his end."

"Better call him and find out what's happening."

Jessica picked up her phone again and dialed Cal's number.

"Jessica? How are you?"

"I'm hangin' in there. Anything happen yet?"

"Not yet and I'm not sure it will."

She gasped. "What do you mean?"

"I mean J.T. Beaumont wasn't the guy. I've got him admitting to hiring someone to stalk me and Kelly, but he adamantly denied having anything to do with Carson's accident."

"And you believe him?"

"I could tell when he was lying before—and he seemed different, like he was telling me the truth."

"Cal! You've gotta do something. I already called Goldini's thugs. If they don't hear something by noon, they said it's off and they're going to add some late fee to the deal."

"Don't worry, Jessica. I've got a few more leads."

"Better get on them fast. We're running out of time or else this thing is going to blow up in our faces."

"Just stay calm. I'm doing the best I can."

She hung up and threw her phone down on the couch next to her. Burying her head in her hands, she started to weep.

CHAPTER 53

CAL'S PHONE BUZZED with a text message from Folsom. It was full of instructions for the types of stories he wanted accompanied by deadlines and word counts for each one.

He shoved his phone back in his pocket before another message buzzed his phone.

Call me ASAP

Cal rolled his eyes.

Now he wants to play nice and be my buddy.

Cal dialed his number. Folsom picked up before the first ring finished.

"Where are you?" Folsom asked.

"I'm not at a strip club, if that's what you mean."

"You're a real comedian, Cal. Seriously, are you at the track?"

"I'm here. What do you need?" Cal wanted to derail the conversation and let Folsom know what frightening things he'd experienced in the past twenty-four hours while trying to chase down NASCAR's story of the decade, perhaps the biggest story in the sport's history. But he decided against it. Too little time.

"I just got a call from Owen Burns."

"The Davis Motorsports Team crew chief?"

"Yeah, that's the one. He said he'd been fired last night but he wants to talk with you about an exclusive."

Cal ran his fingers through his hair and exhaled. "I don't know if I've got time for that, Folsom."

"Make time."

"Fine," Cal huffed.

"I'm texting you his number now," Folsom said.

Cal hung up and stared at the text. He dialed the number.

"Hello?"

"Mr. Burns?" Cal said.

"Yes?"

"This is Cal Murphy from *The Observer*. I hear you wanted to speak with me."

"Yes, I do. Do you have your laptop with you?"

"Will I need it?"

"You need to see what I'm going to show you on you computer."

"What is it?"

"Proof that someone sabotaged Carson Tanner's car—and proof of who it is."

"Where are you?"

Cal jotted down the information and dashed back to the media center to get his laptop. He hustled through the garage before he felt a hand grab a large swath of his shirt and yank him backward.

"Why the hurry?" a familiar voice asked.

Cal spun around to see Ned Davis clutching him by the shirt.

"We need to talk."

***

OUTSIDE THE RACEWAY, throngs of race fans had already begun to clog the ticket turnstiles. Burns walked backward away from the crowd toward the fence. He stood on his toes and looked above the crowd, searching for Cal Murphy.

"Lookin' for anyone I know, Burns?" Alayna French asked as she rolled up on a golf cart.

"I'm tryin' to find Cal Murphy. You know him?" he said still scanning the sea of people.

"Yeah, yeah."

Burns ignored her.

"Too bad about you losing your job and all," Alayna said.

He stopped and glared at her. "How'd you know about that?"

"There's not a story on the infield that gets past me."

"So I've heard."

Burns' eyes suddenly widened and sweat started to bead up on his face.

"Are you all right? You look like you just saw a ghost."

Burns shook his head and reached into his pocket. "Look, find Cal Murphy and give this to him."

"And what do I tell him when I see him?"

"Tell him it's from me—and that it's elementary, my dear Watson."

"Huh?"

Before Alayna could utter another word, Burns vanished into the crowd. She watched as a pair of men in dark suits raced past her golf cart in the same direction as Burns.

***

CAL SQUIRMED AWAY from Davis' clutches and shrugged him off.

"Don't you walk away from me," Davis said.

Cal stopped and turned. He walked steadily toward the owner and stopped a couple of feet short as he glared at him. "Did you think I was just going to ignore what was going on here?" Cal laughed sarcastically. "Not a chance. I know what you've been up to this whole time."

Davis pointed his finger in Cal's face. "What I've been up to is guarding the interests of this team and making sure some rogue reporter doesn't ruin everyone's livelihoods around here."

"Livelihoods? Is that all you're concerned about? What about lives—like Carson Tanner's? You care about that?"

"What's done is done. I can't change the past."

Cal leaked a wry smile. "Want me to quote you on that?"

"For the past week, you've done nothing but make trouble for this team. All you care about are sales and web hits. You couldn't care less about the people's lives your stories are hurting."

"Couldn't care less? Couldn't care less? Are you out of your mind? The only reason I'm doing this is because I actually care about people, starting with Jessica Tanner, who's widowed and pregnant and practically penniless."

"And I offered to take care of her."

"To keep her quiet," Cal huffed. "You think I can't see right through your motives?"

Davis puffed his chest out and wagged his index finger. "And you don't think I can't see through yours?"

"You have no idea what sacrifices I make to track down these stories."

Davis laughed. "Sacrifices? You have no clue what everybody in this organization goes through just to make this team competitive."

"I doubt their wives are stalked and shot at."

Davis stared at Cal, slack-jawed. "What are you talking about?"

"Why don't you ask Beaumont?" Cal slapped Davis on the shoulder. "I'd love to stay and chat, big guy, but I've got a meeting with your fired crew chief. Something about a video I need to see. Later." He didn't wait for a response and turned toward the garage gate.

Cal looked over his shoulder to see Davis busily dialing his cell phone. He knew he didn't have much time.

***

CAL STOOD OUTSIDE the gate on a plastic bunker, hoping to see Burns more easily. Burns had told him he was wearing a red hat and sunglasses along with a black jacket. But so far, nothing.

Where are you, Burns?

"Well, I do declare, if it isn't Cal Murphy."

Cal looked down to see Alayna French wheeling to a stop in front of him in her golf cart.

"Hi, Alayna."

"Lookin' for Owen Burns?"

Cal hopped down from the bunker. "How'd you know that?"

She smiled. "I know everything, remember?"

"Seriously, how'd you know?"

"I just ran into him a few minutes ago. He looked like he was in a hurry, so he asked me if I knew you and requested that I get this to you." She handed him the thumb drive.

Cal inspected it closely. "Did he say anything else?"

"He just said something like, 'Tell him it's elementary, my dear Watson.'"

"What the heck does that mean?"

She laughed. "I don't know. I guess you're Sherlock and you're supposed to figure out whatever is on there."

Cal took the thumb drive from her and jammed it into his pocket.

"Need a lift?" she asked.

He nodded.

"Well, climb on in. We've got a race to get you to."

***

CAL JAMMED THE THUMB DRIVE into his computer and waited for the file to appear. He glanced around the media center, full of sportswriters banging on their keyboards to finish up their last stories before the race festivities began. The pre-race shows blared over the intercom system as several racing experts explained how today's finish would make an impact on the championship race. Outside, it was eerily quiet. Only the droning buzz from the growing crowd and the occasional public address announcement filled the air, which would soon be dominated by the roar of forty-three engines.

Cal clicked on the folder and selected the only file in it.

He watched in disbelief. Then he played the video he sent himself from Ron Parker's phone. It was a match. Only this time, the footage Burns gave him was clearer—so much so that he could positively identify the person tinkering with Carson Tanner's car.

Elementary, indeed.

Cal's phone buzzed. It was Jessica again.

"Well? Anything?" she said.

"Yep, give me fifteen minutes and this is going to be everywhere."

"That's about all we've got," she said.

Cal stared at his keyboard and typed in a few searches. It didn't take him long to find something he'd never noticed before in all his research, something that was now so obvious.

He stood up and saw Eddie Simpson talking to another reporter in the corner. Cal headed straight for him.

"Eddie, you need to see this," Cal said.

Simpson followed Cal and covered his mouth as he watched the incident unfold.

He pointed at the screen. "Are you sure that time stamp is accurate?"

Cal pulled out his phone and started the other video. "It matches the time stamp on this phone. No reason to think two cameras colluded to change the time."

Simpson rubbed his face with both hands and groaned.

Cal remained serious. "I'm heading down to the garage now. Care to join me?"

CHAPTER 54

CAL HUSTLED TOWARD the Davis Motorsports Team hauler with a line of people in tow. He'd wrangled a television cameraman away from his pre-race buffet, while Simpson had grabbed Rick Plimpton, the vice-president of competition, and filled him in along the way.

"I'm not so sure about making a spectacle out of this," Simpson protested, as he struggled to keep pace.

Cal waved him off and didn't turn around. "I thought you guys liked all the off-track drama. Great for ratings, right?"

"I just think there might be a better way to do this," Simpson said.

"I'm sure there is, but not today. By the time I explained to you why it has to happen this way, it'd be too late."

Clutching his laptop in one hand, Cal turned the corner and set his eyes on the Davis Motorsports Team crew. They appeared to be enjoying a plate of ribs, potato salad, and baked beans, while they laughed at some story Dirt was telling.

Jackson Holmes gestured in the direction of the oncoming crew, causing the head of every crew member to spin in Cal's direction.

"Tryin' to make more trouble and ruin this race team an hour before the race?" Russ Ross said. "This is gettin' old."

"Not this again," Beaumont chimed in.

"Not tryin' to ruin anyone's day. But maybe your new crew chief can explain how he ruined Carson Tanner's life last week."

Holmes froze.

Ned Davis stormed out of the hauler and surveyed the situation. "What's the meaning of this?"

Simpson held up his hand toward him. "You'll know soon enough."

All eyes reverted back to Cal. "Go ahead, Holmes. Why don't you tell them?"

Holmes swallowed hard. "I don't know what you're talkin' about."

"Really? No idea? I have surveillance footage that says otherwise."

Holmes' eyes widened. "Footage of what? I didn't do anything."

"I could tell you about it—but I'll just show you." Cal opened his laptop and turned it around so everyone could see the screen.

Gasps emanated from the small circle of onlookers as images of Jackson Holmes using a blowtorch to heat what appeared to be a return spring in a suspicious manner.

Davis feigned outrage. "Is this true, Holmes?"

Holmes hung his head. "I never meant for anyone to get hurt."

Dirt recoiled and went to punch Holmes before Ross grabbed him from behind and pulled him back. "I oughta tear you apart right here," Dirt growled.

Cal closed his computer and shook his head. "When I saw that, I had to ask myself why? Why would anyone want to kill their driver—or perhaps just sabotage their car?"

Holmes' eyes narrowed and cheeks turned crimson. "Carson Tanner was a murderer! He deserved it!"

"You've gone from you didn't mean for anyone to get hurt to Carson Tanner deserved to die in about five seconds. Want to tell everyone here why you did it—or should I?"

Holmes stood up. "I want a lawyer."

"Sounds like a good move on your part because based on all this, you're going to need one," Simpson said.

Plimpton turned toward Davis. "In light of these facts, we're going to suspend your team until we can do a further investigation into what role Jackson Holmes played in Carson Tanner's accident last week."

Beaumont ran up to Plimpton. "You can't do that! This is my shot."

Plimpton shook his head. "If you're good enough, son, you'll get another shot somewhere else. But it isn't going to happen today."

Beaumont turned toward Cal and walked in his direction. He pointed his finger at Cal as he spoke. "This is all your fault. If you hadn't been so hell-bent on bringing down this team, maybe we'd be racing in an hour."

Cal smiled. "Relax, Beaumont. I may have just saved your life, even though I understand your frustration since I doubt you'll ever get a shot on this level again after everything you've done comes out too. And I hate that for you. You really had potential to be a great driver."

Beaumont made a run Cal, who'd turned around and begun walking back to the media center.

Pop!

Cal spun around to see Beaumont flat on his back with Dirt standing over him, fist still clenched.

Dirt tipped his cap to Cal. "Thanks. I had to hit somebody after all this."

Cal nodded and continued toward the media center. He looked at the cameraman who'd followed him. "Did you get all that?"

"Sure did. Are we done yet?"

Cal took a deep breath. "You are—once you get that aired. I've still got plenty of work to do."

CHAPTER 55

CAL SAT IN HIS CHAIR at the media center and pounded out the breaking news. Rick Plimpton gave Cal a quote to add to his story, a story destined to win him an award for spot news reporting.

He called Folsom to tell him all the gory details as he posted the article to the paper's website. Less than thirty seconds later, he tweeted out the link. One minute later, his phone blew up with text messages.

Cal called Jessica. "It's done."

"I know," she said. "I just got a call from them. They're on their way."

"Good luck. You'll do great."

He hung up and scrolled through his text messages, most of which were congratulating him on the scoop.

If they only knew ...

Then he stopped. It was a message from Owen Burns. Burns called several minutes before while Cal was finishing his story and he sent it to voicemail.

Please tell me you got the message

And then another one:

I need your help!

Cal texted him back:

Where are you?

Then the reply:

RV City. I'm texting you my location on GPS.

Then another text:

Hurry. Bring the cops. They're after me.

Cal stared out at the track, bustling with activity for the pre-race pageantry.

Who's after you?

He shoved his phone in his pocket and caught a tram to exit the infield. He hopped off and walked another four hundred yards against the flow of the crowd until he reached the next tram stop.

As he stood in line, he noticed a sheriff's deputy nearby. The deputy approached him. "Cal Murphy?"

"Yes?" Cal said.

"I'm Deputy Hewes from District 2. I saw you this morning down at the office. How's your day going?"

Cal sighed. "Terrible and wonderful—all at the same time."

"Any way I can help you?"

"As a matter of fact, there is. I've got a friend in trouble right now who needs me. He said someone is after him and to bring some law enforcement. You definitely qualify."

The deputy furrowed his brow. "Do you know what this is about?"

"It's got something to do with a story that I just broke, I think. People didn't want this story to get out—but it has."

"Where's your friend?"

"I'm trying to find him now. Join me."

The tram pulled up to the stop. Moments later, Cal was riding next to Hewes headed into the heart of RV city. He explained to the deputy what had just happened and what he thought was going on. The deputy scribbled down a few notes on his pad.

Cal pulled out his phone and tried to find Burns' location.

Hewes leaned over and looked at Cal's phone. "Got anything yet?"

"Not yet." A pause. "Oh, wait. Right here. We need to get off at the next stop."

Cal didn't wait for the tram to stop before he hurdled the safety chain and ran in the direction of Burns' location. He checked over his shoulder to see Hewes was following after him, radioing for more assistance.

As Cal ran down one of the main thoroughfares, he turned right and saw Burns. With blood oozing from several cuts on his face and a tattered shirt, Burns struggled to stay upright on his knees. Once he noticed the deputy, Burns flung his arm behind him. "They went that way, not ten seconds ago." Then he collapsed face first to the ground.

Cal rushed over to him and turned him over on his back.

"Who did this?"

Burns shook his head. "I don't know. They just kept hitting me."

"Had you ever seen them before?"

Burns shook his head again.

Cal scanned the area. "Okay, I'm gonna get you some water and medical help."

He found a medical station a hundred yards away and dragged one of the personnel with him toward Burns.

While Burns received attention, Cal told him an abbreviated version of what happened with Holmes and Beaumont. As Cal finished relaying the events, he looked up and saw four deputies walking behind a pair of handcuffed men in dark suits. As Hewes walked up to Cal, he tipped his cap. "Thanks for the heads up." He reached inside one of the men's pockets and fished out his phone. "Unlock it for me," Hewes said.

Hewes scrolled through the phone until he handed it to Cal. "Does that number look familiar?"

Cal nodded. "That number belongs to Ned Davis."

"Great. That'll give us a good starting point for this investigation." He took the phone back and passed the detainee off to another deputy. "So, Mr.—"

"Burns."

"Mr. Burns, can you tell me what happened?"

Burns adjusted the icepack on his cheekbone. "Where to begin?"

CHAPTER 56

JESSICA TANNER SMOOTHED her hair out and opened the door to the RV. She swallowed hard and stared down at the two men outside. They scanned the near-desolate campgrounds and ascended the steps.

"Mrs. Tanner," the first man said as he tipped his black bowler hat. The second man followed him inside without saying a word.

She sat down.

"I'm Bill," the man said. "Gary here is gonna take a look around, if you don't mind."

Sweat beaded up on her face as she shook her head. "I don't mind at all."

Gary stumbled around and opened every door he could find, including the cabinets.

"I see the news convinced you," Jessica said.

Bill laughed. "I wasn't sure what to believe."

Gary nodded at him and gave him the okay sign. Bill then held out his hand, palm up. "Where's your cell phone, Mrs. Tanner?"

"Right here," she said, reaching for it on the table.

He snapped his fingers. "Give it here." He threw it down on the ground and stomped on it a few times.

"What are you doing?" she asked.

"Just makin' sure you don't call the cops after we leave." He rubbed her head and then sat down. "No hard feelings." He adjusted his suit coat. "So, let's get down to business."

"Before we do, I want to know how Carson got tied up with you."

Bill laughed. "No big deal. He was just lookin' to expand his meager winnings by betting on some games here and there. He got a little behind. He told us he was going to pay us once the season was over. I'm a patient guy, but I knew I'd get nothin' if I didn't act now." He paused for a moment. "And Mrs. Tanner, I want you to know I'm sorry for your loss. I actually liked your husband."

A tear trickled down Jessica's face. "You have a funny way of showing it—threatening his widow."

Bill waved his hand dismissively. "Ah, I don't threaten. I promise to do something and take action. Threats are empty." Then he threw his head back and laughed again. "You don't climb to the top of this world making empty threats; you climb it with action."

She wiped the tear away. "That's funny. I was always taught you rise to the top with a combination of hard work, integrity and good fortune."

"Work is the only thing that matters in your little trifecta. We all make our own fortunes, good or bad. So far, mine has been pretty good." He took a deep breath and put his hands on his knees. "So, shall we get down to business or what?"

"Fine," Jessica muttered.

"Do you have the money I asked for?"

"And what exactly is this for again?"

"Look, lady, I don't need to spell this out for you. I already told you what it was for." Then he stood up and glared at her. "Are you wearing a wire?"

Gary lunged at Jessica and ripped at her shirt. She tried to withdraw, but it was too late. Two buttons on her blouse popped loose, exposing not much more than an inch of black wire snaking around her bra. But it was visible—and that was enough for Bill.

Bill grabbed her hair and shoved her toward the door. "Let's get outta here now."

As they descended the steps of the RV, an FBI SWAT team surrounded them.

"Drop your weapons," one of the agents shouted.

Bill ignored the command. Instead, he shuffled along the edge of the RV with his gun pressed firmly into Jessica's head.

"Nobody has to get hurt," Bill said. "Especially the little lady here. Don't you think she's been through enough this past week."

"Just let her go," the lead agent yelled.

"Or what? You won't arrest me?" Bill cackled. "Pardon me if I don't trust you."

***

CAL STARED AT HIS PHONE that now seemed to vibrate constantly with alerts that new messages had arrived. He scrolled through them and smiled. It had been a while since he'd broken a story this big and it felt good, a feeling he imagined was about as high as winning a championship for the athletes he covered.

With just fifteen minutes until the green flag dropped, Cal found himself as the tram's lone passenger. Every serious race fan—which would be everyone on site—was already seated inside the raceway. Cal paused for a moment to make small talk with the tram driver. Then he returned to scrolling through the messages.

But when the tram slowed down unexpectedly, Cal looked up to see the driver staring into RV city with his mouth agape. Cal turned to see two men slinking away from an FBI SWAT team, all with weapons trained on the men. And the men had a hostage. His stomach sank when he recognized who it was: Jessica.

She looked over and saw him. "Cal!" she screamed.

The two men stopped. The man holding Jessica cranked his neck in the direction of the tram. "Hey, you, driver guy. Stop. I need to borrow your tram."

The driver followed the instructions. He parked the tram and left it running, fleeing into RV city.

Cal jumped up to follow him.

"Not so fast, buddy," the man said. "You're going to join us."

Cal watched as the SWAT team lowered their guns and took no action.

Still clutching Jessica, the man slid onto the same row as Cal. "Nice to meet you, Cal. I'm Bill." A pause. "I'm the man you need to listen to if you want to live."

CHAPTER 57

THE TRAM LURCHED FORWARD and Cal stared at his feet. He couldn't bear to look at Jessica after he'd gotten her into this mess. Half an hour ago, he experienced one of the greatest highs in his career. Now, he thought it was all a worthless endeavor, especially if it meant the end of his life or Jessica's.

Bill remained quiet as Gary drove the tram toward an unknown destination—at least to Cal it was unknown. Cal went over scenarios in his mind about where they might be headed. With miles of dirt roads in the valley, they could be headed anywhere. And wherever they were going, danger would lurk, that much Cal was sure of.

After ten minutes, the tram stopped.

"Let's go," Bill said.

By this time, he'd lowered his gun, holding it in Jessica's back instead of to her head. Gary jumped out of the driver's seat and rushed over to help Bill corral the two prisoners. Gary grabbed Cal by the arm and led him forward.

"Let's move it, you two," Bill growled.

They walked toward a Chevy Silverado with an extended cab and tinted windows.

"This is perfect," Bill shouted. With his free hand, he

pulled a small device out of his pocket and jimmied the door open. Cal and Jessica climbed into the back of the cab before Gary zip tied their hands together.

Bill then took off his jacket and grabbed a t-shirt from underneath the seat. He dug around in the console and found a pair of beat-up sunglasses along with a pack of Marlboro Lights.

He laughed again. "This is better than perfect!"

Once everyone was secure in the truck, Bill hotwired the engine and pulled onto one of the perimeter roads in RV city. He drove slowly and took a deep breath once he saw the exit, manned by a Maricopa Sheriff's Deputy.

"No way out now," Cal said.

"Shut up," snarled Bill. "There's always a way out. If you say one word, I'll shoot the both of you and this dopy deputy."

Bill rolled his window just over halfway as he approached the officer.

"How are you gentlemen doing today?" asked the deputy, who couldn't see deep into the truck.

"Doin' good," Bill said as he forced a smile.

"Any reason you're leavin' while the race is about to begin?"

"Beer run!" Bill said as he turned and high-fived Gary, who was getting into character.

The deputy cocked his head. "You are aware that there's a Safeway grocery store on the premises, aren't you?"

Bill nodded. "Yeah, but they're out of Natty Light."

"And you didn't come for the race?"

"Of course, we did. But we really came to party!"

The deputy stepped back. "I need you to step out of the vehicle."

Bill threw his hands up but remained seated. "What for? We haven't done anything wrong."

"I just want to make sure you guys haven't been drinking too much."

"Well, all right," Bill said. He kept his hands in the air where the deputy could see them—but it didn't matter. Bill lunged at the officer and grabbed him by the back of his shirt before slamming his head into the door three times. The officer slumped to the ground.

"Hurry up, Gary, and give me a hand," Bill said as he scanned the area. Cal looked around to see if anyone had witnessed what just happened. No one else was around.

Cal slumped back into his seat.

"What are we gonna do, Cal?" Jessica asked.

"I—I don't know," he mumbled. "I'll think of something. Just don't panic."

"Don't panic? Don't panic? Don't panic?" her voicing rising an octave each time she uttered the phrase.

Cal watched as Bill and Gary finished moving the deputy into his car and positioned his hat over his face like he was taking a nap.

"Look, just calm down," he said. "Here they come. Just be cool. We'll figure this out."

Bill jumped back into the truck and roared west on Indian Springs Road, which ran parallel to the track. They continued in silence for about two miles until they came to the edge of Estrella Mountain Park. The road veered right and Bill drove on until he slammed on his brakes.

Cal lunged forward and hit his head on the back of Bill's seat. When Cal looked up, Bill's face was inches away from his.

"Move outta the way!" Bill barked as he looked over his shoulder and rammed the truck into reverse.

Cal leaned back and to the side to view a roadblock about a hundred yards down the road. Then he peered behind him to notice two black Suburbans blocking the road to their rear.

"Everybody hold on," Bill said.

Cal drew his knees up and tucked his head between them, gesturing to Jessica to do the same.

Wham!

The truck rammed into the two Suburbans as the steel crunched and squealed on impact. The tires screeched and burned while Bill kept the accelerator pedal to the floor to get all the way through. After a few seconds, the truck shook free and sped backward away from the roadblock.

Cal watched several FBI agents with their guns trained on the truck, but they didn't shoot.

One violent turn and the truck now faced in the opposite direction, headed on a gravel road into the backside of Estrella Mountain Park.

"What have we got here?" Bill asked.

Gary scrolled on his phone. "Keep going. Just ahead on the right. It's a horse park."

"Excellent!"

Cal looked through a trail of dust toward the former roadblock. He could only hope the FBI would come after them before something really bad happened.

CHAPTER 58

THE TRUCK SKIDDED to a stop and Bill and Gary hustled out of the truck. They pulled open the doors and yanked Cal and Jessica with them.

"We've gotta move," Bill barked.

Bill stormed into the Western Corral Park's office and brandished his firearm. "We need two horses now," he said.

The woman behind the counter swallowed hard. "Okay. Follow me."

"Don't try to be a hero, lady," Bill warned as they walked.

She led them outside to a stable with about twenty horses by Cal's best estimate.

"Got any saddled and ready to go?" Bill asked.

"This way," the woman said as she led them toward the end of the stable. A stable hand, listening to music through his ear buds, brushed one of the horses. When he looked up to see the two gunmen dragging a pair of hostages toward him, he dropped his brush and dashed away.

"Make sure he doesn't do anything stupid," Bill said.

The lady nodded.

She approached one of the horses and handed the reins to Bill. He hoisted Jessica onto the horse first before jumping up behind her.

Gary shoved Cal up onto the horse before climbing up behind him as well.

The woman stared at them. "Now, I need to tell you a few things about these horses—"

"Save it, lady," Bill said. "We're not interested." He looked around the stable. "Are these all your horses?"

She nodded.

"I want this entire stable opened up right now. I don't want any of the feds coming after us on these horses. Got it?"

"Yes, sir."

She didn't move.

"Do it now!"

She scrambled down the stable, opening each gate to release the horses. In a matter of moments, Bill and Gary were at the reins of two horses ahead of a growing stampede.

Cal clung to Gary as the horses climbed the rocky terrain and headed deep into the park.

The two assailants rode along in silence. It seemed eerie to Cal, like they'd either done this before or were communicating some other way. It spooked Cal, whose stomach grew queasier with each passing minute.

After thirty minutes of traversing along the mountain-side, Bill led them toward a dry gulch. With a patch of trees, it provided the most cover in an otherwise open terrain.

"You need a break?" Bill asked Gary.

"I'm good. Let's keep movin'."

Cal glanced around and noticed a rattlesnake coiled up just a few yards ahead on the right. He took a deep breath before speaking.

"Can we stop? I have to pee," Cal said.

Bill stopped his horse and turned and glared at Cal before producing a dramatic eye roll.

"Did bitty bladder drink too much today?" Bill said. "I'm surprised you haven't pooped your pants yet."

"I'm serious," Cal pleaded.

"Let's keep moving." Bill turned and continued along the gulch.

"No!" shouted Gary. "I'm not gonna have this dweeb takin' a piss all over my back. Let the man go." Gary halted his horse.

Bill stopped too. "Fine then. Make it quick."

Cal climbed down off the horse and eyed the rattlesnake just a few feet away from Gary's horse. He slowly walked in the direction of it.

"Will ya hurry it up?" Bill growled.

"Okay, okay," Cal said as he increased his pace.

He took a deep breath and then kicked dirt in the direction of the snake. The snake rose up and headed toward him. Cal shuffled around, placing the horse between him and the snake. As Gary tried to figure out what was going on, he turned his horse around until it was facing the snake.

Gary's horse then reared back, tossing him hard to the ground.

Bill watched slack-jawed. "What the—"

With his hands still tied, Cal scurried over to Gary, who wasn't moving. He used the terrified horse, which was bucking about, as a shield from Bill. Cal snatched the gun off Gary and pulled a knife off his belt before he tiptoed away from his co-rider, who still lay motionless on the ground. Cal sawed discreetly at the ropes on his hands. He then began to slowly back away from Gary once he saw

306 | JACK PATTERSON

movement out of the corner of his eye. The snake returned and slithered toward Gary.

"No!" Bill yelled, shooting at the snake.

He missed. The snake recoiled and bit Gary on the neck.

Bill leapt off his horse and started to run toward Gary. He didn't even see the gun trained on him.

"That's far enough," Cal said, his hands shaking.

Cal walked sideways, keeping Bill in front of him. "You can tend to your friend, but you're going to let us go."

"You know I can't do that," Bill said, reaching for his gun.

"Keep your hands right there," Cal said. "I know how to use this thing."

"I doubt that," Bill said.

With that, Bill's hand darted toward his gun, but it never got there.

Bam! Bam!

Cal put two shots in Bill's left leg. Bill staggered to his knees and then fell over on the ground.

However, he didn't lie there for more than a second or two when he heard the clicking of the rattlesnake behind. Bill wobbled to his feet and limped away from the snake.

"Now put your gun down and kick it over here," Cal said.

"Are you crazy? I'm gonna need this thing."

Cal fired another round at Bill's feet.

Bill put his hands up. "Okay, okay. Here." He followed Cal's orders and kicked the gun to him.

Cal kept his gun trained on Bill while he picked up the other one and jammed it into the back of his pants. He then backed toward Bill's horse.

"Give me your hands," Cal said to Jessica. He cut her free. She didn't need any instructions to know she was to do the same to him.

Cal climbed onto the horse behind Jessica.

"Good luck, Bill," Cal said as he grabbed the reins. "You're gonna need it."

Cal directed the horse out of the gulch and toward the hill they'd just descended. Once they reached the top, they saw several law enforcement agents on ATVs. They rode down toward them and told them where Bill and Gary were. One of the agents peeled off to escort Cal and Jessica down the hill toward their response unit to get a full report.

For several minutes, neither of them said anything.

Jessica cried softly and sniffled.

Finally, Cal broke the silence. "I'm really sorry about all this."

Jessica shook her head. "It's not your fault. I'm just glad it's over." She burst into more tears. "I still haven't even properly grieved Carson's death yet."

"Grief is something that never really goes away," he said. "You just learn how to handle it better."

She nodded. "It's just that I feel like I found out I was married to someone I didn't even know."

"Carson was a good man—no matter how or why he got tangled up with these guys. Don't ever think differently about him. Make sure your little girl knows what a good man he was."

She sniffled again. "It's just so strange. I never knew that side of him—the side that would be reckless to involve himself with people like that. He was always so careful, so safe. He even double-checked his race car before every race. It just doesn't make sense."

"Everybody has a past, but I've learned it's always better to give someone the benefit of the doubt. People can change, you know?"

She nodded and didn't say another word.

The roar of the engines droned in the distance.

CHAPTER 59

CAL NURSED A CUP of coffee and watched Kelly read his story. He smiled at every slight change of expression that swept across her face.

"Are you kidding me?" she asked as she put the paper down, mouth agape. "Talk about plotting your revenge."

He nodded. "I almost missed it. After observing the team and listening to all the rumors, I was convinced it was anybody but Jackson Holmes. Even when I saw the video, I didn't believe it."

"There has to be more to the story than what you ran."

He smiled and nodded. "Always." He took another sip of his coffee and stared out the window.

Kelly snapped her fingers. "Hello? Aren't you going to tell me the rest of the story?"

"If you insist."

"Of course, I insist. Now quit keeping me in suspense."

"I found most of this out after I wrote the story—or I couldn't properly source it. But as with any murder like this, I'm always looking for the motive. And that's clearly why I missed it. There didn't seem to be a clear motive for Jackson Holmes. He was a new guy to the NASCAR scene and appeared to be content just to get his shot as a crew member in the big leagues."

"How long had he been with the team?"

"Just two years—which makes you think if he was going to do something, why wait two years, right?"

Kelly nodded.

"So, anyway, what I found out was that the Goldini family had a strong grip on several different levels of racing. They'd pay off guys to throw races or to wreck favored drivers. But they were smart enough to only do it on occasion. However, there was a driver named Scooter Jones on the K&N East circuit who told the Goldinis that he would wreck the pole sitter that week. I forget who it was, but it doesn't matter. Then, Jones went out and won the race."

Cal took another sip of his coffee and continued.

"This really irked the Goldinis. They told Jones that he owed them two hundred thousand dollars, and Jones reportedly laughed at them to their faces. The Goldinis then went to Carson Tanner and told him he needed to wreck Jones hard within the first five laps of the following week's race. Tanner owed the Goldinis a favor after they had the favorite eliminated a few months before to clear the path for Tanner to win his first race."

Kelly's eyes bulged. "Wow, what a tangled web this story is."

"That's not the half of it. So, Tanner wrecked Jones hard, causing serious injuries. After ten days in the hospital, Jones died from injuries due to the wreck." Cal paused. "And guess who is cousins with Scooter Jones?"

"Jackson Holmes?" Kelly said.

"Bingo. I almost missed that in his bio, which made a brief mention of it. And I still probably wouldn't have thought much about it until I typed in their names together. The second search page had a big story about the death of stock car racing's next greatest hero who would never be—and both their names were in the article. Jackson Holmes was quoted and he seemed miffed, to put it mildly."

"But Davis Motorsports still hired him?"

"Maybe they didn't see the article. I don't know. It's not like Ned Davis would tell me anything these days. NASCAR suspended him from operating a team for two years."

"The cover up is always worse than the crime."

Cal nodded. "And the crazy thing is, he didn't commit the crime either. He got what he deserved. At least for him, he's not facing a murder charge like Holmes."

Kelly folded the paper again. "Have you spoken with Jessica since you got back? How is she?"

"She's fine—and the baby is fine. Her baby still needs that surgery, but it looks like she's going to at least be able to get that life insurance policy to pay out now."

Kelly's stopped. "Do you hear that? Sounds like Maddie waking up." She darted off to get her daughter.

Cal drained the last of his coffee before his phone rang. It was Owen Burns.

"Burns, how are ya?"

"Alive—and employed."

"Congratulations. Who'd you land with?"

"I can't talk about it right now, but when I can, you'll be the first to know."

Cal smiled. "Thanks."

"No, I'm the one who needs to be thanking you. You salvaged my reputation and career with that article. Davis had already done his best to marginalize me—and if you

didn't have the courage to do what you did, I might be looking for some other type of work."

"And that'd be a bad thing?"

Burns chuckled. "Probably not, but racing is all I know.
And I love it with every fiber in my being. So, I just had to
tell you 'thank you.' "

"My pleasure," Cal said. "Be safe out there."

"Don't worry, I always am."

Cal hung up and watched a few rays of sunlight beam
through the naked trees in his backyard. He understood
Burns' desire to stick with his passion. It's what drove him
to be the best journalist he could be.

Buzzz.

Another text message?

It was the tour chaplain, Burt Glover.

I told you it'd work out.

Cal nodded and put his phone in his pocket.

Yes, you did.

His phone buzzed again.

Geez, what is going on?

It was Folsom.

Speak of the devil. Wonder what he wants?

ACKNOWLEDGMENTS

THIS NOVEL wouldn't be what it was without the help of the good people at the Phoenix International Raceway. Their help was invaluable in helping craft a story that could be considered both realistic in setting and scope.

Zac Emmons, the public relations director at PIR, was a tremendous help in getting me access to the track and drivers. Aimee Dulebohn, one of his team of consummate professionals, was also a big help to me while in Phoenix.

While I might feel like a true NASCAR driver in the number of people I thank, it really did take all these people to help me write a realistic story about a story so many people are passionate about. Justin Allgaier, Kurt Busch, and Jeffrey Earnhardt all took the time to talk with me about their experiences on the track and off of it to help create more realism with the people surrounding racing. Glenn Evans, Ryan Scott, and Manny Leach are some people who work tirelessly behind the scenes to help create such great theater during the races — and they all were gracious enough to take time to talk about the sport they're all so passionate about.

Lauren Emling, Alex Taurus, and Rory Connellan all

helped make those interviews with drivers happen, and for that I'm incredibly grateful. They also shared with me their experience around the sport along with Amy Walsh in creating a big picture and their role in the drivers' lives.

When it comes to those who helped me with the novel, the usual suspects abound, but I first must acknowledge you, the reader, for fueling my passion to write these stories.

Jennifer Wolf once again helped make this a better story with her deft editing skills.

Dan Pitts crafted a beautiful cover that captures the mystery and wonder of where this novel took place.

Bill Cooper continues to crank out stellar audio versions of all my books—and I have no doubt that this will yield the same high-quality listening enjoyment.

I also want to thank Duncan Campbell, one of my readers who over Twitter suggested that I write a story using NASCAR as the backdrop. That kind of interaction with Duncan is one of the reasons I love writing in the new digital age as no author is forced to write in a vacuum any longer.

As always, I must acknowledge my wife for allowing me the time to write this story and to spend time away from our family researching and writing.

And finally you, the reader — thank you for your support in my work. It inspires me to keep writing.

ABOUT THE AUTHOR

JACK PATTERSON is an award-winning writer living in southeastern Idaho. He first began his illustrious writing career as a sports journalist, recording his exploits on the soccer fields in England as a young boy. Then when his father told him that people would pay him to watch sports if he would write about what he saw, he went all in. He landed his first writing job at age 15 as a sports writer for a daily newspaper in Orangeburg, S.C. He later earned a degree in newspaper journalism from the University of Georgia, where he took a job covering high school sports for the award-winning *Athens Banner-Herald* and *Daily News.*

He later became the sports editor at a daily newspaper in south Georgia before working in the magazine world as an editor and freelance journalist. He has won numerous writing awards, including a national award for his investigative reporting on a sordid tale surrounding an NCAA investigation over the University of Georgia football program.

Jack enjoys the great outdoors of the Northwest while living there with his wife and three children. He still follows sports closely.

He also loves connecting with readers and would love to hear from you. To stay updated about future projects, connect with him over

Facebook: facebook.com/JackPattersonAuthor
Twitter: twitter.com/MrJackPatterson
Instagram: instagram.com/mrjackpatterson/
Web: www.IamJackPatterson.com